GRAY SPACE

K. LEE

GRAY
SPACE

GRAY SPACE

THE CROOKED KITCHEN

I ain't never been a girly girl. I don't wear tight skirts, booty shorts, or skinny jeans. It's all really uncomfortable to me, and I don't know why people would buy this, knowing how it feels on your skin. I don't want nothing that feels glued to my crotch, either. Maybe I am slightly autistic. I am not really sure. I was never tested.

If you come from a proud black family, you probably wouldn't get tested for a lot of things. People will just call you different, and for us, that was good enough. I don't think I need drugs because I don't like clothes clinging to my skin. I just learned to deal with it.

I swear that when people say we moved forward with the feminist movement, I would say it didn't apply to all of us. Before, it was illegal for women to wear pants, but now, if you don't wear something tight, people think you are a dike or something. I hate the term because it is offensive to us women who like alternative clothing. Just because we like alternative clothes doesn't mean we live an alternative lifestyle.

I have to shoot so many women down who come

on to me. I used to get mad and frustrated, and then I started doing my nails just to prove I was all woman. Now, I just laugh and call these women thirsty. I wear baggy clothes because I don't want a yeast infection, to be comfortable, and able to breathe, but women can sweat you harder than a dude sometimes.

I could go on and on about this topic. I think I should have been born in the 90s or something when girls liked big clothes, and it was cool. I wouldn't put a condom on my eye like Left Eye. I still think that was wildly bold. But we are here now. I know you didn't come to hear me talk about lesbians and dikes, so I will get to the story.

My name is Rain. Not sure of what my mom was thinking. I think she was into some R&B groups or something. So many old-school music videos she likes got rain in them. So maybe she was thinking, "Rain would be dope?" But I'm not sure; I guess that, too, doesn't matter. My mom is cool, though, and she is a '70s baby whose social life took off in the '90s. She was very sheltered growing up.

I am an only child, not because I didn't have siblings. Hearing the question, "Got any brothers or sisters?" still bothers me. I've been to more funerals than I care to remember. So I don't wear dresses, and I often wear black. It is not because I am a goth, but maybe I am in mourning or something. I've heard that a few times from a street therapist and my mom.

You know, everyone has an opinion about what's wrong with you, but no one really knows. I started going to church when my baby brother died. I believe in God, and honestly, if I didn't, I might have been the third dead child. I did everything possible to keep away from the streets and anything looking like it.

Living in the hood doesn't keep you more than an elbow's reach away from trouble. So, I feel my less appealing look keeps people from looking at me. I never wanted to be desired and get entangled with gangs. So I really dress like this for protection. I know it might be weird, but that's me.

I have been on this job for about six months now, and I don't think these managers give a dang about nobody. They run this place like we are slaves. They talk all crazy, and although they don't call us the "n" word, they know they can't, but that don't stop them from denying any days off you request.

I have tried to get days off because I was sick, and they said if I don't come in, don't bother coming in tomorrow. I mean, what kind of job is this when you cannot get a day off that they don't assign to you? I don't like the control they have over people. I can't wait to leave.

But I know better than to quit a job when you don't have one. I cannot sit at home and make no money, this world don't run off good hearts and ideas, unfortunately. It runs off money, and you need it to pay bills. I hate missing church every Sunday. I go when I can, but that isn't often.

My mom wasn't religious when we were growing up, but she has gotten better after both my brothers died. I think she thinks like I do: maybe they died because we didn't go. We haven't had an issue in a decade with the cops or gangs. Same house, but a whole lot less drama. I didn't talk much about my father.

He doesn't come around much, never really did. He didn't have an easy life, but he chose that. He was selling weed when he was young. When my mom found out, she got away from him quickly. But she was already pregnant with me. My older brother's dad was killed selling drugs, so she didn't want a repeat. My younger brother's dad is in jail for robbery. He never saw him born or spent any time with him.

My mom thought it was a bad idea to take him to the jail. So when he got old enough to go, that's when bad news struck, and he was killed before they could come to visit. My mom has really been heartbroken, and although I want to save up money and leave this place, I don't have the heart to leave her.

She loves this city and it is her home. I pray we can take a vacation this year because it would be so well deserved. Maybe we can go somewhere hot and sunny, like Jamaica or something? So, we gotta work and make the money.

I try to stay under the radar, and I must say, I have been doing a great job. Staying under the radar means being at work. Right now, I am at work getting things out of the freezer, nothing new. We have to prep the kitchen mad early, and this was one of those days we all hated and wanted to end quickly. I never complained about the work because it doesn't change nothing. I try to blend in, and I do a good job of not voicing my opinions on anything.

I see how people are quick to throw you under the bus when they think you about to get to the top. It is like crabs in the barrel, and you can't trust nobody. So, don't jump into fights that ain't your fight.

I grab the tray of fresh produce to start cutting and getting things together. It was uneventful. Cutting lemons is a no for me without gloves. I hate having sticky, ashy fingers. I am a bit of a neat freak, and that's my mom's fault.

She always kept a clean house. Growing up, we had assignments, but my brothers weren't much help. My older brother was slow, and if you ask me, lazy, and my baby brother never got to the point of doing anything more than taking out the trash. Cooking and cleaning, I guess, I learned from my mom.

She has been a cook and a house cleaner since I was young. She has worked for the same family, it feels like for decades. I don't know if she has ever cleaned for anyone else. She leaves early and comes home in time to take care of us. Her job, I would say, is flexible. She could always get to our school when we got in trouble or we got sick.

She has always been an active parent in my life. She was like a mother and father when it came to both nurturing us and disciplining us. We didn't have close relatives nearby that she cared for us to connect with. Her mom and dad were never together growing up. She and her mom argued a lot, so we didn't see the two of them together much either.

She loved her mom, but said she couldn't be around her long. She drank and smoked most of her childhood, and I don't think she ever got past some trauma. She felt something was best not said, and poking the subject was like me poking a bear. I gave up and just let it be. I know when someone doesn't want to talk, so I let it ride.

My mom was stubborn when it came to stuff she didn't want to do, but she was quick to mind her own business. This is a trait you pick up in the hood to survive, too, I guess. You don't jump in when you are not invited to the conversation. So I cut up the lemons and wash my hands. After, I go back into the freezer and go to pick up a tray of chicken, and something falls to the floor.

I look down to pick it up and it's a ziplock bag wth something in it. I didn't pick it up, but went to put the chicken down on the counter first. I went back into the freezer and I looked closer at the package. I don't understand how a baggie with anything other than food got into the freezer.

The package was slim, but it looked like a ziplock bag with driver's licenses. What would that be doing in here? I picked up the package now that I knew it wasn't drugs, haha. I guess I watch too many movies. I live in the hood, but I have never seen drugs other than weed.

My mom once found some in my brother's room and made it a house meeting. We never saw anything like it since that conversation and beat-down she gave my brother. I had nothing to say; we were all scared of my mother. Who needs gangs when you got an OG right here? She simply didn't play.

I brought the items out of the freezer and could better see the images in the packet. It was an ID for someone who didn't work here anymore. I thought maybe he left it behind, and I should bring it to the office. Only when the bag shifted around there were other IDs in it from another person I hadn't seen for a while, either.

It was strange enough to find one ID, but to find multiple IDs from people who didn't work here anymore was strange. I wasn't too sure if I should bring it to the office just yet. I am no detective but I watch movies, like I just said, so I grew curious. Why would they hold people's IDS?

I overheard a few people complaining about some underhanded stuff happening with the managers, but I didn't have a clear picture. Some of the IDs in the bag were people I remember working with here. I wasn't sure why everyone got fired or left. One day they were here and the next they were gone, often with no excuse. I didn't ask questions, but now, looking inside this bag, I wish I had.

So I did something I said I wouldn't do: ask questions. I went to a coworker and asked about one of the people in the bag. He said they transferred to another store. When I asked him which store, he said he didn't know. He just came in to work, and the managers who had the answers were already gone. He had to do double shifts often, so him being rude was normal. I hated him at the pass because everything was intense and full of yelling, like we worked for the British Man on tv.

I didn't think long on the bag. It could have been dropped, so I wasn't too bothered. I just knew that it meant I should keep a lookout for other people who spontaneously quit. I started to ask more questions in case it might do me some good later. I started to make friends more and say simple things to keep a line open with everyone.

For the most part, that month was uneventful, but then one day, someone who I knew wouldn't miss a day was gone. I asked around to see what happened to him and called his personal cell. He replied, "Man, those bosses up there are shady. Be careful and don't trust none of them."

"What's going on? They fired you?"

"Something like that, but basically, I am getting transferred to another sto'."

"Which one?"

"Trust me, you don't want to know."

"You going to be working with Inez?" I heard she got transferred, too."

"Like I said, the less you know, the best."

Of course, I didn't ask any more questions, at least at that time. I kept my ears open and overheard the ladies talking in the bathroom. I doubt they knew I was in there. The servers usually hide out in the bathroom before their shift and vape if they can. I pulled my legs up, hoping not to be heard, as they kept on chatting.

"Hey, I saw your man didn't come today?"

"Yeah, this place is something else."

"How they found out?"

"Yeah, he smokes weed, but it's legal everywhere. Why should that be such a big deal? They jump at the chance to blackmail anybody. You heard about Inez, right?"

"Not the whole story."

"She got into a fight with her boyfriend, who was using. Of course, his supply is Jazz, and the boss heard she pulled out a gun."

"Dang, she did that?"

"Yeah, bad part, she's on probation. She can't get caught with no gun, or she is going straight back to State."

"So what did he do, Jazz?"

"He said if she didn't take this job, he was going to rat her out for distribution."

"I told her to stop messing with that dude. He was using and passing out everywhere, getting stupid. It was only a matter of time before she was going to have to pull a gun on him. She should have left drugs alone, period, when you got too much to lose and you ain't making money, just ain't worth it. Inez's man was messy. She should have cut him off. She was just getting her life back. Plus, she got a baby."

"But if she slips up, Jazz ain't going to protect her. She's gonna exchange a possible gun charge for a drug trafficking charge? She already got two strikes. She's playing rushing roulette."

"You already know Jazz is gonna look for the quickest way to sell off anybody to protect what he's doing. She's sold up the creek; everything she was trying to do with starting over will be gone."

"Wow, that's wild. I told her, leave that dude alone and have nothing to do with people who on that shit."

"You can't save everybody."

The room just got smaller. The ladies left out, and I sat there for a couple of minutes more. I knew they would be looking for me on the line. I've heard there were people doing drugs, but I didn't think it was something big. How did Jamal get caught up like this? Was he selling drugs or worse, using?

I wasn't sure what to do, but I couldn't sit in the stall anymore. I came out and went to start my shift. Jazz came up to me and asked, "Hey, I think I lost something in the freezer. You see anything?"

"Like what?"

"Just did you see anything that wasn't food?"

"Naw, I don't think so." He left without saying thanks. I wasn't sure of what was going on but I wanted to help Jamal. Maybe this bag could be leverage or help him and Inez. But how could I tell him I found it? I went to look at the schedule and his name wasn't listed. How did they pull him so quickly from the schedule?

Around here, getting a day off was unheard of. So I flipped through a few more pages looking to see if anyone else was removed. I got to the back of the schedule and found something strange. His name and Inez were listed. Why were they listed in the back and not in alphabetical order?

I looked at the top of the sheet, and the header said vacation. I thought it was an error, but I wanted to ask a manager to find out what they would say. Stephen walked past me and I said, "Hey Steph, where's Jamal? He was supposed to help me get through with prep."

"Aw, he is out sick. I think he should be back in tomorrow. Sorry about that. Let me know if you need help." He didn't mean anything he said, and I know he is lying. I finished out prep and worked my part of the line. I worked saute and made salads mostly during my shift. I was efficient and quick, so I didn't mind it. When my shift ended three hours after I should have left, I called back up Jamal on my way home. I was curious of what else was in that bag.

I didn't go through it before, but now I think I should. I had plans to tell Jamal. "Hey Jamal, you sick?"

"Naw, why?" he replied.

"Oh, I asked about you and they said you were sick."

"I told you, Little Momma, stay out of this." This nickname he picked up because he says I can be a bit bossy when I am planning prep. There is so much to do that if I don't organize the responsibilities, we ain't finishing. So we trade off and do what we do best. I cut the onions and do the stuff he doesn't like, and he takes care of the meat and stuff I don't like.

"Jamal, I want to help you. What's up?"

"I don't know if you can."

"What do you need? What have you gotten your-self into?"

"I don't do drugs no more like that, but I had one slip up, and they drug tested me. I failed. If that got reported to my p.o. It's back to the slammer for me, and I ain't going back."

"So what you gotta do?"

"Stay at home for now, was what they told me, Rain."

"But on the sheet, it says you are on vacation."

"Yeah, they took my ID and stuff, so I can't move."

"I might have that."

"How you get it?"

"Long story, but Jazz was looking for a bag I found in the freezer. It might be in there."

"Man, if you get me that, I will disappear. Them dudes say I'm on vacation, huh? They probably draining our holiday pay and days off. I never got a paid day off. If I had a day off, I had to come in or get fired. And I never got that money."

"So you think that's why you and Inez are still on

the schedule?"

"Inez?"

"Yeah, I checked the last paper, and it says that you two are on vacation. Nothing about you being fired."

"They didn't say I was fired, but they told me I had to sit at home."

"That doesn't make any sense. I heard the waiters in the bathroom talking, and they said they got proof that Inez pulled a gun on her boyfriend."

"How they get that?"

"I don't know, but they threaten to rat on her if she didn't transfer. Something about drugs."

"Man this some bullshit. They know I ain't selling no dope no more. I am clean, I promise. I went to a party and it was there. It was one line, but I am not back on that shit. I ain't going nowhere near it."

"I can give you the bag, but what's that going to do if they think they got something on you?"

"I don't know. I really don't understand right now what's going on."

"I can see what I can find out."

"Be careful, and I really don't want to ask for you to get caught up in this. This all sounds foul, Rain."

"I ain't doing nothing illegal, so they don't got

nothing on me."

"Be careful still. It sounds like they're making up stuff or looking at people they can spy on. You would think they got enough out here in the streets going on. What they need me for?"

"I don't know. But I will try and find out."

I got home and I checked the contents of the bag. It was several people's ID, social security card, and direct deposit details. I know I should give Jamal back his stuff, but if I do, he is going to tell them I had it. Worse, he might leave and I won't see him any more. That can't be good for probation.

I needed to figure out what was going on and see if I could give a story to the cops. I know we not supposed to involve them, but I won't have no other choice. I just needed to understand what was going on so I could help. I needed to snoop.

I went to work the next day, and the line was quiet. It was different with so many people gone. We used to have six people working the line, and now we only got three at a time. The others supposedly transferred out, even though they were still on the schedule.

I called Jamal back to see what was up, and he said he got offered a job at this club. He had an easy job, security. But he said they took half of his money because it had to go to insurance. I told him he was still on the schedule at work, and he told me they told him not to come back up there.

I asked Jazz, "Hey, is Jamal better? He's been out a

few days, and I am still doing prep myself. I see him on the schedule."

"Yeah, he transferred out. He won't be back."

"Really? So why is he scheduled to work today?"

"It might be a typo or something. I will get it fixed. "

"I also saw Inez on there and a few other people who aren't here."

"Yeah, you heard something else?"

"Jamal and I were close, but he said nothing about transferring. So I just think it's odd he's gone and ain't called me. I should probably call and check on him."

"If he wanted to talk to you about it, I am sure he would have called you. People leave all the time, Rain. You are not anyone's momma. It's no big deal. This is the restaurant business." I didn't say anything, but I guess I did a look he didn't like. "You got something else you want to say, Rain?"

"No, just curious why people are on the schedule who aren't coming in when this helps us to know what to expect for the day."

"Do you need a day off?"

"You firing me?"

"You keep asking questions that don't have anything to do with you. Why are you so noisy?"

"Jamal was my friend, so we looked out for each other. If he left me hanging, he should have said something, is all."

"Rain, I am not dealing with this. I think you need to go home before you say something you will regret."

"Look, I ain't trying to cause no trouble."

"You already did. Go home."

"But who's going to work the line?"

"I will figure it out. No one's irreplaceable. This is just food." I shook my head, took off my apron, and headed out. I was a bit nervous when we were talking, but he looked guilty. He acted like I knew more than I did. I went out the door, and I was grabbed by the shoulders.

"Hey, don't be scared. We need to talk to you."

"What, get off of me. I don't know you." I backed up and said, "What's up? You robbing me or something?"

"No, I am DA agent Teresa Martin. I need to talk to you."

"What's that?"

"District Attorney's office. It's about your managers." I followed her and she checked to be sure we weren't being tailed. "I know you are on to something about these guys. What have you found out?"

"Honestly, I don't know what I found out. Some of

my friends and ex-co-workers are getting blackmailed. I am not sure what's all happening, but a lot of them are being transferred."

"Transferred to where?"

"They are forced to work at this club, but their names are still on the schedule. It looks like they are on vacation and are even working a schedule, but they don't come in."

"Alright, we know more than you, and that is a good thing. If he fires you, let it ride, and we will take care of the rest."

"But what about my friends Jamal and Inez?"

"If they want to cooperate, I am sure we can get them a deal."

"The people who need jail time are Jazz and Stephen."

"I can't make promises, but I know the people who can. Let's see what they can do, but you stay far away from this as much as you can. We like to say we can protect people, but we can't guarantee that. The less you know, the better. Go in tomorrow and quit your job."

"Quit?"

"Yes, say it's hard working here and give your reasons. Make it good so they don't think nothing. They might have thought you were working with us already. So don't make them think that at all. If you stay, they won't trust you anyway and I fear what they are capable of."

Great. I am out here playing "Double o' Negro", and now I don't have a job. My mom is cool, but we got bills and are working to take a vacation somewhere. I don't want to let her down. I wasn't expecting to lose my job.

TELLING MOM DUKES

I got home and walked in with my head hanging down. My mom was sitting on the couch, and she barely looked up from the tv. I went into the kitchen to get something to eat. You can't tell bad news on an empty stomach.

I work in food, but I never wanted to eat there. I guess I get tired of seeing the same things all day. There was nothing wrong, I just lost my appetite for fish, salads, and soup. I wanted a home-cooked meal, and like clockwork, my mom had something on the stove.

She worked early so she could get home early. She would start her day at like 6am and be home by 3:30pm. She didn't like driving; cars made her nervous. She was in a real bad crash and never got over it. So she never taught me to drive either because she said they were dangerous.

I am twenty-four and still don't know how to drive a car. One day, I will get around to learning how. So she takes two buses to get there and comes home the same way. I can count on my hands how often she got a ride. She just doesn't like cars much.

I grabbed my plate from the microwave because it was still hot. Mom cooked meatloaf, peas, and mashed potatoes. One of my favorites. I think she definitely has some kind of sixth sense going to pick up what I got going on. She knows what to do, even when I don't.

I sat at the table, and I felt her come in and rest her hands on my shoulders. "How are you doing?" I replied back with not much enthusiasm. "It's going."

"Now, I know for sure something is up. What's going on?"

"My bad, Ma. The food is good, thank you. I had a rough day today at work. I've got two weeks, and I need to find something else."

"I knew this day was coming. You can't get in-volved with everybody's life, Rain. " She let me take a few more bites of my food and said, "Rain, you gotta mind your own business. You can't save everyone, and what ain't your business, you need to leave it alone."

"You don't think I should have gotten involved?"

"Who is losing out right now? You or the people you are trying to help?" I didn't say nothing, but I saw what she meant. I kept eating, and things were silent. She was right, they all had some kind of job or circumstance. I am the one out here with nothing, trying to figure out a way to pay bills. Right now, times are hard to find a job. No one is hiring, and a lot of places are closing because people are still scared to spend money.

I hate recessions because everyone cries broke. We can pay for these app places, but when it comes to sitting down and enjoying a meal, this is a dying art. How am I going to get a job in this? I hit the computer to look for a job. I knew I was on a timetable to get something else.

I went into work the next day, and I complained to Jazz. I knew how to shift the direction, or at least I thought I did. "Hey Jazz, I don't want to work here no more. I've been thinking about it, and I think it is time to do something else. Doing prep by myself is hard, and people are on the schedule and won't come in or whatever. The schedule is supposed to let us know what's going on and who's scheduled, but nobody's here. I am doing the job of like three people, and I am dying."

"So that's what yesterday was about? You working the line alone?"

"Yeah. I've been coming in by myself, people don't show up, I don't get days off, and now I see everyone getting days but me. There is a lot of work, and the work keeps piling on for me. So, I'm done."

"You sure you want to do this? Getting a job right now is hard, Rain. I would hate to lose you. You are one of my best employees. We really need you here."

"Nobody's irreplaceable, right? I thought about that and it hit me, I gotta do something I am passionate about, too. I really don't want to do this anymore. I am thinking of going back to school and doing something else. There isn't enough money in this."

"What if I could offer you a job where you can make more money and not deal with food?"

"Nah, I want a desk job. I am done with anything in the kitchen, a restaurant, or hospitality. But thanks for thinking of me."

"Alright, I will keep you on the schedule in case you change your mind. Take the next few days and think about it."

"Alright, thanks." What kind of job could he be offering, I thought, but didn't ask. I was getting out of here before things I thought would happen got any worse. I did keep thinking about what he said though, he would keep me on the schedule. Is there something special about keeping people on the schedule? I wonder if they get bonuses or something for who works and how much they earn.

Maybe that is why no one seems to quit but leave and stay on the schedule. Maybe they are doing something funny with timesheets? I worked the extra two weeks, and he kept pressuring me to stay. Each time, I respectfully declined, and I saw many people on my list still on the wall. I was leaving the company, so I thought it would be no problem to give Jamal his ID and what else I had for him. I don't know why I didn't think to give it to the agent. So I will call her to give the stuff to her to figure out. I don't want it tracking back to me.

I asked him when I saw him again, "Is something funny happening with timesheets?"

"Why do you ask?" DA Agent Martin said.

"It's nothing, maybe. I just thought it was odd that people would transfer, quit, or get fired, but they stayed on the schedule."

"That was something we noticed, too. I can't tell you too much for your safety and because this is an ongoing investigation, but you are on to something. Keep that to yourself."

I left out the office and I was at ground zero. I was looking for a job, but it was hard to work anywhere. I know getting employment was always a challenge, but this job market was next level. My mom saw me sitting at the table on the computer and doing all I could. One day, she sat next to me and asked a question.

"How would you feel about working with me?"

"What do you mean, Momma? I can't charge you for doing stuff around the house."

"Dang right, you can't. I meant working with the family I work for. They are private people, so you gotta keep your mouth shut about your opinions. But if you show up and do what you are told, you can work an easy job making good money. I've been there for years because I can't complain about nothing."

"Okay, what would I have to do? Help you clean?"

"No. Actually, they just fired the personal help for the mother. She has dementia, Alzheimer's, or something like that. She forgets a lot of things. She can use the bathroom and do things herself; she just forgets to eat and do stuff. So they want someone to come in and make sure she is good."

"You sure I should? I mean, she doesn't know me. Isn't it good for her to have a familiar face?"

"No, I don't think it matters. She only remembers one of her sons and her dead husband. He died years back. If she remembers anyone else, that's a miracle. So you won't hurt anything. I can give you the instructions on what to do. You come in, cook the food, wait for the next meal, do it again. Then you make dinner and leave afterward. Her son comes home to feed her dinner."

"Okay, I mean, the job seems easy enough."

"But I need you to understand that anything you see in that house stays in that house. You don't see anything, hear nothing, and you keep loud headphones around your neck. Put them on if you ever need them."

"Oookay. So, when do I interview and meet the family?"

"I can take you to work with me tomorrow."

I slept like a baby knowing I had a job in the bag. Life gets a bit gloomy when you are hunting for a job and can't catch a break. I went to the interview and I did dress up. I wore a dress, something I did about three times a year. The times are Mother's Day, Christmas, and Resurrection Sunday.

Getting on the bus was annoying, seeing everyone stare at me, or at least it felt that way. The ride was uneventful as we pulled up to her house after leaving the second bus. I don't know how my mother did this for years and made it look easy. I am not going to be choosy because I need this job. I put on my best informal smile because smiling too hard made you look thirsty. I don't know, I feel like if someone is smiling real hard for a domestic job, it could give the vibe you want to steal.

So I played it cool and waited to be greeted. My mom came in and quickly disappeared. She told me to sit on the couch, and someone would be down to speak to me. I sat there and I looked around the room. The house was immaculate. It smelled wonderful and looked expensive. I don't know where they were getting their furniture from, but it was certainly not from a store I have ever been to.

The legs on the furniture were a brilliant gold color. The couch was stone heavy. I accidentally bumped into the leg before I sat down. I wore heels so infrequently that even these wedges gave me trouble. I quickly plopped down sideways on the couch as it broke my imminent fall–I hoped no one saw me. I thought I was in the clear.

Around the corner came a young man smiling. "Hi, is it Rain?"

I stood up to shake his hand and replied, "Yes, that's right. Hi, how are you doing?"

"Doing great. So your mom told us about you, and I would love to get to know you. If you are like her, I am sure this will work out."

"Thank you." I couldn't give the cliche response, "She told me nothing but good things" because she didn't say much but to do my job and mind my business. I couldn't say that, so I tried to avoid saying anything further about that. To change the subject, I said, "You have a lovely house."

"Yes, my mom designed it. I think she could have been an interior designer if she would have went to college for it."

"Sometimes life can be that way when we get busy. What does your mom do?" I asked.

He does a low cough and says, "Oh, yeah, she is well retired now. She has an onset of dementia that doesn't allow her to work or remember much. She was forced to retire. It's kind of funny she doesn't remember anything about her past but me and my father."

"Oh, but you are not an only child, right?"

"Right, I have an older brother, James. Oh, my bad, my name's John."

"I won't forget it. So my mom said you were looking for a cook?"

"Uh, yes. We are looking to have someone cook three meals for my mom. My brother and I are in and out, but for the most part, I live here, and my brother pops in when he feels like it. I will be here for dinner, but I am not always here for breakfast and lunch. I was never big on breakfast, even if I was here."

"Okay, so three meals a day. Should I just make enough for you to eat lunch, so when you are hungry, you will have something?"

"Yeah, that would be cool. Thanks for asking. One other thing I would like for you to do is to keep her company. She doesn't have friends or family, just my brother and I. I don't want her to get lonely during the day. We are a private family, so if you could keep whatever she may say private and tell no one, that would be great."

"Of course. No problem. Last question, any

dietary needs?"

"Right. No, she is fine to eat anything, but we want her to have a balanced diet. Are you good at making a menu?"

"Yes, I can do that. If you like, I can show it to you for your approval–"

"No need. When can you start?"

"Yeah, yeah, um, I can start as soon as you need me. I am flexible."

"Good. If you like, you can run with me to the store, and we can get what you need for the week. I can take you to the store, or you can get the card and get what you like."

"You can drive. I don't currently drive."

"Right, so you don't drive either?"

"Nah, my mom's been real strict on that for me. I usually take the bus everywhere."

"That's no problem. I don't mind going with you. What size shoe do you wear?"

"Oh, a size 6 1/2 or 7."

"Good, my mom might have some shoes you can wear."

"Oh, that's okay. You don't have to do that."

'It's my pleasure. I saw you on the camera. Those shoes can't be comfortable to stand up in. I'll go grab them."

I could swear he had a muffled laugh as he walked away and up the stairs. I guess I wasn't alone, and eyes were on me. They must have cameras all over this place. He must have been watching me to see what I did while I was waiting. Good thing I am no thief or opportunist.

I switched out of my shoes and went to the car. We arrived at the market and I shopped for what I always wanted to cook at the restaurant. I bought salad items to diversify the meals. I did look up ingredients that were healthy for people with dementia and brought urban staples in the mix. I think the menu will bring nostalgia mixed with a healthy balance.

He didn't talk much, but he watched for everything I picked up. It's kind of strange to know you are being supervised, I guess. When we got to the checkout counter, the groceries were rang up, and he whipped out his card to pay. He dropped a heavy black card that felt nothing like my card. It thumped against the mini counter, and he quickly put it away. The other card in his hand, he gave to the cashier, a normal-sized card. She swiped while having casual conversation.

She was a bit flirty with the eyes if I am honest.

He paid her no mind and started to help gather the groceries into the cart. When we arrived to the car, I said, "I think she likes you."

"Everyone likes you when they see you've got money. I don't pay these women no mind. Not my type."

"I hear you. You can't trust many people nowadays." I replied.

"Good help is hard to find is what they say, too." He jokingly said.

As we got into the car, I replied, "So, what happened to the previous cook?"

"She got caught stealing and sleeping with my brother."

"Oh."

"Yeah, whatever you do, don't steal, don't lie, and mind your business, and we should be good. If my brother hits on you, please don't sleep with him. Tell him you are not interested, okay? Keep it professional, and I will back you up."

"No problem." I went back to the house, and my mom was still working room-to-room, cleaning. It was apparent someone in this house must have been OCD. The house was super clean, and I don't know how she had cleaned the entire house daily. I didn't ask the question then, but I would when the time was right.

I put away the food, and John disappeared after giving me a quick tour around the kitchen. It had the touch of my mom, so finding things wasn't as difficult for me because I knew her system. It was a bit odd that I had been working this job for a few hours and I still hadn't met his mother, my actual client. I do think that is important, but just so I am not a stranger to her.

I am not sure if they were not too worried because she had dementia. All I could think about was if she would like me or not. I cooked the first meal which was white sautéed fish, and a strawberry, spinach, and quinoa salad. Of course, I jazzed up the seasoning and kept away from dairy. I wanted to eat a plate myself because it looked so good.

I didn't have a phone to call John, but he popped up at the right time. "Hey, I meant to give you my number. Let me see your phone." He input his number: "Call me if you ever need something."

"Thank you. It's all ready."

"Okay, let's go meet my mother." That was it; he didn't tell me anything about what I was about to walk into. He didn't mention the food, so I wasn't sure if she would like the food. John had taken the tray for her himself. I poured her a glass of water, and as a backup, I had a low-sugar juice in case she wanted that. I wasn't sure if she liked tea, but I guess I could ask when I saw her.

The stairs seemed to go on for a bit before we reached the top. They needed an elevator in this place for real, or I needed to get into better shape, probably. Working in food, everything is at your fingertips, so there are no stairs involved. Thank God for these shoes, or my feet would have certainly died a long time ago.

Along the wall were pictures of a family with a lot of single portraits or photos. I saw maybe one group photo, which I thought was strange for the family to be so close. I would have thought children's photos and married pictures would be everywhere. But the walls were decorated with art instead. The art seemed original by the signature and apparent brush strokes. I am no scholar, but the work looked good.

I asked John, "Hey, so who did the art on the walls?"

"I did." He replied.

"Really?" I was impressed.

"Yeah. What? You don't think a black man can paint fine art?"

"No, honestly, I just, well, I wouldn't know fine art if I saw it."

"You saw it, and you did recognize it. I think you are doing pretty good." I took a deep breath in and he said, "Relax, I am just playing with you. I started painting when I was a child."

"Long time, then?"

"Yeah, my mom supported me in this. She would post my paintings on the fridge and I was so proud. She made me want to keep painting all my life."

"So, what you painting now? " I asked.

"Let's pick this up later." We reached her door, and he tapped two times before opening it. "Mom, we are here with your food."

The room was lowly lit as if the curtains were drawn closed. It was too dark for me to feel comfortable in the space myself, so I am glad he was there. She must have been in her bathroom because I didn't see her when we entered.

Her room was gorgeous, though. That same gold from downstairs was carried upstairs. She had fur rugs and stools. Her color scheme was white and powder blue marble with silver and gold accents. She had white everywhere. You can tell no children lived here.

Her room was spotless. Maybe she is the reason the rest of the house was so clean, too. This house was so big, I can't imagine her cleaning all of this by herself. Heck, I don't see how my mom can clean this in a day. It wasn't a speck of dust anywhere as I looked at the dancing chandelier over my head. It was silver and gold-plated with sparkling crystals.

It didn't look cheap, and I was sure it cost a good fortune for them to live here. From my days of shopping online for my future house, I saw some of the light fixtures and some of them I knew cost well over two thousand dollars for the smaller units. What kind of money does this family have?

I looked around but tried to look casual so as to not alert them of my curiosity. I think John was a good judge of character, which is likely why everyone met him. I didn't want to breathe wrong. I needed his mother to like me, and I was praying to God that she would.

I heard the toilet flush and knew any moment she would be emerging from the doorway. I took a deep breath, and John said, "Sit down. It might be better if we both were sitting." I quickly sat down and looked down to my shoes. I thought, Oh man, will she realize I was wearing her shoes? Will that be good or bad for me?

Sometimes people get upset when you take things that are theirs, even if they hadn't worn them in a while. I think John felt my nerves and said, "Relax, she doesn't bite. She can be firm but she is cool once she gets to know you. Just be yourself and you will be fine. I pray we are not scaring you?"

"No, no, I am fine. Just nervous whenever you meet someone new, you know?"

"Yeah, I get it."

"Mom, we are here, and Rain is here to meet you. She is your new cook. Come out, woman, what are you doing?"

"I am coming, just getting presentable. You should have told me someone was coming, John."

I did, Mom."

She snaps, "Are you getting smart with me?"

"No ma'am."

"Be respectful, I raised you better than that."

"Yes, ma'am, you did," he said jokingly.

The doorknob rattled, and this snappy woman was about to come out of the door. I thought I would be less nervous after sitting down, but my nerves grew like a group of dancing butterflies breaking into flight in separate directions. Keep it together, Rain. She is just a woman and may love you.

Right, I thought. I am a good person who has always respected my elders. She will love me. The door opens, and the ray of light pokes in from the bathroom.

MEETING MY CLIENT

Before entering the room, she says, "John, open the curtains or turn on the light." He gets up and quickly draws back the curtains. The light was well welcomed in the room. I think that was what was wrong the most about the meeting. It felt like we were meeting in the dark.

She walked in wearing her bedroom slippers that were name brand and, of course, gold in color. She wore a lush white robe with silver silk pajamas. Her hair was colored and in an updo; she didn't look a day over 45.

She was a beautiful woman, and you can tell she never saw an ugly day. Some people go through an ugly phase before they become beautiful, but this woman didn't carry herself like that at all. She looked me in my eyes with her hazel green eyes and said, "Hi! How are you?"

"Oh, I am great, ma'am."

"You don't have to call me that. Call me Brittany."

"Thank you, Brittany."

"Don't I know you?" She asked as she turned her head slightly sideways.

"You do?" I asked, slightly puzzled.

"Yeah, we met years ago. Your name is Felisha, but we all called you Fancy, right?"

"Fancy?" I replied confused, but before I could correct the misunderstanding she said.

"Yeah, don't you remember?"

"Ugh–" Thank goodness John bailed me out and replied the right thing to say.

"Yes, Mom, she remembers. But that was a long time ago. She came to bring you your food. Fancy works with us to help make food and keep things around the house."

"Oh, baby, thank you. I appreciate that. What did you make for me?"

"I made a strawberry, spinach, and quinoa salad with sautéed white fish."

"Oh, you are fancy. I haven't had quinoa before. What is that like? Rice?"

"Something in that family. Maybe a bit softer and a similar shape. It is a good brain food."

"Yeah, that isn't as sharp as it used to be. Thank you. I will try to eat it. Bring it to me." John stood up to bring her plate, she said, "No, not you John. I want Fancy to bring it to me. Did you need anything else?"

"No mom, I just wanted–"

"She is my old friend. My eyes are not that good, but I see her clearly now. I know her, and you are good to leave."

"I will be by later to check on you," he replied before leaving.

"John, you don't have to come by so often. I am okay. I'm not dying."

"Mom, please don't talk like that."

"Hell, it's true. I remember what I needed to know and the people I needed to know. So don't worry so much, will you, John?"

"Sure, Mom. Enjoy dinner." He looks toward me and says, "Rain-Fancy, when you are done, can you come down and speak with me?"

"Yeah, of course," I replied, relieved that she liked me so far.

He exited the room, and his mother said, "Fancy, tell me, how have you been?" She unwrapped the napkin and placed it gently over her lap. She was a proper lady. I looked at her and said, "Things have been okay."

"Oh, so do you have children? A husband?"

"No, umh, no. I don't"

"Marriage is wonderful. You should get married and find the right one. My Robert is so good to me. I am surprised he hasn't called already for me."

"I can see how that could be nice."

"Oh, marriage is wonderful. Hot nights with your husband are the best. I am no perfect woman, but my husband made me honest, you know. I will always love him for what he did for me. Don't you date, or have children, or something?"

"What do you mean?" I asked?

"I figured you would have had a family by now. We all can live the lives we want to. Have you met Robert yet?"

"No, I don't think that I have. How did the two of you meet?"

Brittany's Flashback...

It was back in the seventies when bell-bottoms were in, big afros, and the streets were busy with activists, street runners, party-goers, and people who wanted to have a good time. My mom told me I was fast and looking for trouble when I would sneak out to hang out with my friends. She thought that I would end up in a place I didn't want to be. She was an uptight kind of woman, likely because of this white family.

We had long family ties with this white family. She was the maid, of course, but from the first day they saw me as a young child, they took a liking to me. My father was gone a lot, so I didn't see much of him, and if he had abandoned our family, I wouldn't have known any different. My mom never spoke about him much, and he would just pop up on the step at random times, drunk.

I heard later on that he was a petty drug pusher, nothing major. He was doing whatever he could to hustle up a few dollars. He didn't keep a job was what I overheard when staying up listening to my mom and her friends gossip about their lives. He seemed like a deadbeat, and I guess that was why my momma kept me away from him.

I didn't know if what they were saying was true, and I prayed that it wasn't. I wanted a dad like how the white family's had. They looked so happy, and I thought maybe we could have that too. My mom's neighbor would watch me when my mom worked. On this cold day, my mom's friend's heater went out. It was freezing in her house, and she didn't think it was safe for us to be there when her pipe burst and water started gushing everywhere.

I was like six or seven when this happened. I was scared. We tried to stop the water by turning off what we could, but it didn't help. It was a main line burst in the wall so water soon started to spread throughout different areas of the house and the building. She called my mom at her job, and she said she would be there.

Before she could explain everything to her employers, the wife offered to drive and pick me up. Up to this point, she had not seen me before. My mom pulled up at my friend's house, and she rushed up to me to check if I was okay. I was fine, we were standing outside for awhile so my fingers were bright red.

The white lady saw my hands and took off her gloves. She put my hands in them and said, "Rub your hands together and, Brittany, blow on them. I would hate for this child to catch frostbite." Her gloves were so soft. I don't know if it was because I couldn't feel my hands or not, but they felt like magic. I had never had gloves like these before.

They were dark gray leather cashmere gloves that I loved. My mother nursed me in the back while the white lady drove. I knew that was a sight for people to see. She didn't complain the entire drive, and I prayed in the backseat that I would cause no trouble when she was at work. My mom was big on manners and not acting ghetto. She was big on you becoming who you want and not being conditioned by your surroundings.

We arrived to the house and it was gorgeous inside. The furniture was well organized. The pictures on the walls had no dust, the baseboards shined. You could eat off the floor it was so clean. My mother told me to go in and sit at the kitchen table, and I did as she told me. I kept my coat on and the gloves the white lady gave me.

I didn't see my mom for what felt like hours, so I laid on the kitchen table and drifted to sleep. I woke up to someone tapping me on my shoulder. "Hi, baby. Are you still cold?"

"No ma'am. I am not cold." At this time I started sweating because her house had heat. She helped me take off my coat and said, "Are you hungry?" I was but I wasn't sure of how to respond. "It's okay, you can tell me."

"Yes, ma'am. Just a little bit." She went into the fridge and started getting me something to eat. I was nervous while she did it because I didn't know what my mom would say if she saw it. She came in and seeing the lady work to feed me, she said, "Oh, no, ma'am. I can do it, no need."

"No, Missy. I insist. It is alright. I want to do this. You can do what you were doing." My mom looked at me, but it wasn't a rude look. I knew I wasn't in too much trouble as she walked out. The lady started talking, "Do you like peanut butter and jelly sandwiches?"

"Yes, ma'am." I replied.

"Good, I will make you that."

"Thank you so much. If you need me to do it, I can make it."

"No, it's quite alright. I can do this." She busied herself making the sandwich. It took much longer than the time my mom took. The bread was from a fresh loaf of bread. The peanut butter spread like magic, and the jelly tasted like it had real fruit in it. It was the best sandwich I've ever had. I wonder what kind of food was they getting that tasted so much different than ours?

She talked to me at the kitchen table for what seemed like hours. She laughed with me, and she didn't even notice that my mother was done cleaning. I knew I was keeping her, so I said, "I think I have to go ma'am. We have to catch the last bus."

"Oh, where are my manners? I can drive you home."

My mom came and said, "No, ma'am. We can't ask you to do that. Please, we can take the bus. Our neighborhood this late might not be right. But thank you sincerely."

"Right, of course." I started to put on my coat, and the lady picked up the gloves and said, "You keep these. At least once a week, can you come by and see me?"

I looked at my mom, and she said, "Of course she will." I kept coming to that lady's house for years. She taught me all that she knew about decorating, fine taste, eating high-class meals, and place settings. I thought it was like dressing up for a tea party, and it was fun. I didn't pay much attention to what all she said until I grew older.

In the 70s, what was easily hidden became to be more apparent to me. This nice white lady was an escort, and the home she had was a house where many women lived at. I didn't see them when we had come before because they were all sleeping when my mom cleaned. She never tried to talk me into anything, but I would ask, how did she afford everything she had?

She would say, "I had to sacrifice. I didn't have a silver spoon in my mouth, but I was blessed with good looks, men like me, and I used what I had to get what I deserved. Don't you think I deserve fine china, good food, a big house, and to live like a queen?"

I laughed and said, "Of course you do, Nancy." We were on first-name terms at this point. She would come and pick me up, take me to clubs with her, and show me what she did to meet high-class men. She would point to them and tell me who to stay away from. She was quick to let me know, "Stay away from the overly aggressive men. The sex was rough, their attitude flaky, and they could beat on you for no cause."

The number one thing she would say to me over and over again, "Never let a man pimp you. We don't do this for them; we do this for us. They say they offer protection, but we don't need that. We have our own protection." She showed me her weapon, a twenty-two tucked in her purse a few times. I knew she carried, and she knew how to use it.

She repeated it so often, "Never let a man pimp you, ya dig?"

"Yes, Nancy. I dig it."

She told me how to spot them and what I needed to do to attract them. I wanted to learn everything she knew. I wanted to be a queen and live how she did.

I never told my mom that this woman was the reason I was sneaking out, but she caught on. She was pissed off at Nancy, and it was a nasty breakup. They were close friends, too, but my mom didn't like that I was walking in her footsteps. She didn't understand things the way Nancy and I did. She saw it as a disgrace. We saw it as a means to an end.

I enjoyed the clothes, the lavish lifestyle and I knew I would land the right arrangement to set myself up. I didn't plan on living at her home; I wanted my own house. I looked at the other women living in their bedrooms, and I knew that was going to be short-lived.

I needed to scope out what was around me and make the best plan for catching the biggest fish. I wasn't turning tricks forever. My momma did teach me that I had value and I was special in more than one way.

That night at the club, Robert came in. He was quiet and sat in the corner. All the girls were coming up to him, and I knew that wasn't the way. I turned away every trick that came to me, and I kept glancing at him. I knew he saw me a few times. If he had an interest, he would come to me–and he did.

Back to day...

She started laughing and smiling as she reflected on her sentiments. She continued her story.

Flashback continued...

So, he walked over to me with a coined walk from the 70s. I didn't say a word, I just looked at him as he limped toward me. He said, "What's the skinny, Foxy?"

"Watching you," I replied with enough interest and mystery. Men liked this kind of thing.

"Groovy. So what you into?"

"What you got for me, baby?"

He opens his hand and shows me a packet of white powder. I had never seen it, and I knew better than to take it. "I don't do smack."

He takes a seat at the table and looks intently at me, "Fo sho. So what do you do, Foxy?"

"You know."

"I figured. So why you not making your money?"

"I ain't got no pimp. I work for myself."

"So Foxy, you are a businesswoman?"

"Yes. I can take care of myself and think for mself."

"I like that. But look, baby, I ain't making no promises."

"You a Casanova?"

"I dig ya. I ain't looking for love and I ain't making no promises. But if we can work together, and have some fun, we both can be happy."

"And money?"

"You hip, I can dig it. Let's get out of here." He leans in and nibbles at my neck and whispers in my ear. I smiled and he said, "Let's go." I got up from the table and we started walking.

"You gon' be my Foxy Lady," he said as I could feel him watching me move. As I walked in front of him, he grabbed my butt and spanked it. I know all the girls had their eyes glued on me then, and I was a target in their eyes.

That night, we became a team and I did everything I could to keep him and learn from him.

Back to Present Day...

"When we walked out of that place, I knew right then he would be mine. I picked him first, but he responded. Yes, I was a prostitute for a few months, but I quickly shifted when things could make sense. My mom thought I would be in a place I didn't want to be in, but I made it. She would shit on herself to see that I live better than that white woman."

As she reflects, her eyes grew distant when she says, "My mom never came to see me growing up. She didn't care how much I had or where I moved to. She never came by. She cut me off."

She continued, "Meeting Robert, and that memory never left me. I don't remember all the other details, but I remember us meeting and the feeling in my heart. He was a great man to save me, and I will always love him and be his Foxy Lady."

My phone rang, and I looked at it, it was John calling. Brittany thought the call was for her and said, "Is that my phone?" She started looking around the room.

"Can you help me find my phone, please?" I started looking around the room with her. I didn't know how to tell her that her phone wasn't ringing. Then my phone stopped ringing. "Dang, I missed it. That is the thing about getting old. You don't know where you put stuff."

Her plate was cleared, and she was drinking the

last bit of her water. "Thank you so much, Fancy, for the food. It was wonderful. Make that quinoa again sometime."

"Of course. Let me get that downstairs."

"Please, I don't do bugs." I picked up her tray, and she got up and started looking around. Her eyes were wandering long before she did rise, I presume, looking for her phone. I came down to the kitchen, and John was waiting on me. "Hey, I want to tell you thank you for staying up there."

"Oh, of course. It was good to hear her talk."

"She does that a lot. But she is sweet, right?"

"Yes, I do like her."

"Good. Well, I am guessing you are hungry? I am sorry, you are more than welcome to make yourself a plate when you cook. I ate all that you made, my bad. It was good. I can take you to go and pick something up on your way home if you like?"

"Thank you. I am starving." I would have normally said, "No thanks" to a ride. I never liked men knowing where I lived, but I was too tired to walk and too hungry to go another 90 minutes. That bus would have been an easy hour and a half commute. I got something from the nearest burger joint, and he told me to eat while I was in his car.

I was scared because the interior was white with

black trim. It was a gorgeous car and still smelled new. I knew he spent some money on it. I said nothing as I enjoyed the breeze blowing in my hair. I wanted a car like this someday, but today, I was glad not to be walking. I felt spoiled, and I prayed this effect would last. Sometimes, on a job, the best day is the first day, and it goes down from there.

I pulled up to my apartment building and got to thank him before going inside. Of course, as I crossed the parking lot to my building, Keisha was outside. She is a young sixteen-year-old girl who thinks she is twenty-two. Her mother tries hard to keep her inside, but she is destined to break free. Some kids have life so easy, but refuse the easy road.

Her mom is a single mother and she breaks her back to provide for her daughter. She is an only child who has everything she needs but is not satisfied. Her greedy nature has her outside when she should be indoors listening to her momma. I see her and she gives me a sneaky look.

"I see you, Rain. What you doing coming out that fine-ass car this time of night?"

"Cool off. I am just getting off work." John takes off before she gets any closer.

"Why he pulling off like Batman? He got a secret identity or something?"

"Naw, he is low-key. He ain't looking for anything you got to offer if you catch my drift."

"So, he's gay or something?"

"I don't know all of that, and it ain't my business. But I got a suspicion he might be interested in something you are not. Like an adult. You are a kid and you need to have your butt in the house."

"Oh, so you got jokes. I am grown and I do what I want to do. I can take care of myself."

"Really? So if your momma put you out right now, you could take care of yourself?"

"I would learn. I know there is money in the streets and I don't have to wait to go get it. I am gonna come up and make it out the hood."

"Why don't you go to school? Get a paying job that doesn't mean losing your clothes."

"Relax. I ain't no hoe."

"Okay."

I kept walking toward my door as she tailed me to my door. "I pray you don't stay outside too long. This good weather is nice, but it won't be around for too much longer."

"I hear you, Ms. Rain. I am going to show y'all I ain't no dummy, and I got a plan."

"Okay. But just remember, there is money and problems out here. Don't ever think you gonna get something for nothing. The streets always wants something in return, and you bets be sure you can pay up."

"I got it. I ain't gonna do nothing stupid."

"I pray you don't for your own sake and your mother's."

"Why you gotta bring her into this?"

"Your momma prays for you every Sunday. Do right, Keisha."

"I hear you." In the distance, her friends call her back, "Yo, Keisha. We bout to go."

"Okay, I will catch up with ya'll later." The girls leave from outside the building and head toward a flashy car.

I see the situation and reply, "So those are your friends?"

"It's not what you think."

"Sure. I ain't no rocket scientist, but those girls don't look like they work in a lab. Don't run the streets with girls like that. They gonna get you caught up. They in the fast lane, Keisha. Go home and find something you like to do. Use the internet, hell, to find something you love. You can go into coding, banking, use computers to make money."

"Girl computers are taking over the world.
There are only a few things in life that is old, tested,
and true: Men love women, and they will work for
them. If I play my cards right, I won't have to work."

"Are you being serious, Keisha? You sound as
dumb as those girls look getting into that car. Please
think about what you doing and saying."

"If you want to judge me, go ahead. But I don't
want be no chef or no maid. I want a life, Rain. This
is not life. We are in poverty, and nothing is getting
us out unless we make a way. You just don't understand. Life is getting expensive, and these regular
jobs don't pay enough. So I gotta do something,
Rain."

"You ain't listening. But my feet hurt and I am
tired. Night."

"You sounding too old."

I jokingly laugh and reply, "Mind your business.
Heels ain't meant for working in, but sitting down
for me. You can have all that. Go home and tell your
mom I said hi."

She sucks her teeth and says, "Yeah, yeah." She
walks off and I enter the house. I don't think I was
ever this tired from working in the restaurant. Wearing heels does up the game on how you feel.

I used to want to work in an office, but now I
don't think I want torture devices on my feet all day.

I was quick to take off the shoes he gifted me, and although they were expensive and nice, my heart wanted my beat-up and comfy monster slippers. I don't know what makes them so comfortable, the tattered fabric or the memories.

I was in a warm place in my heart. I reflected on the love story of Brittany and Robert, and I liked getting to know her. I am still curious about her oldest son, who I haven't met yet. Something tells me he is a hound when it comes to women.

So, I ain't in no real hurry. I just want to know what I am dealing with. As I wound down to relax, I did what I do sometimes: I went and got into my mom's bed and watched tv with her.

She is my best friend and I wouldn't change it. We don't have to talk, we can just be in each other's presence, and that is enough. She asked a few questions about my day, but I gave her the highlights.

I don't want this family's life to become our bond. I like leaving work at work unless it impacts my life in a direct way or my mother's. We both were good at breaking from the conversation as laughter roared out of our mouths watching tv.

It is the simple things that make us love life. Not having my brothers around at times like this was what hurt the most. We would all pile into my mom's room and sit wherever we could fit and laugh with her.

I am sure she misses the noise, and the company. That's why I laugh a bit louder than before and sometimes roll around her bed to take up space. Seeing her smile and laugh, brings back happy memories for the both of us.

CRASH COURSE
INTO FAMILY

Waking up to go into work wasn't hard. I like the mom, and the youngest son was thoughtful, to say the least. He hasn't been around much lately, so mostly I have been keeping his mom company. I wonder if she ever wants to get out of the house? It seems a bit stuffy to stay inside all the time.

It came to my mind to ask John what he thought about field trips and things to do outside the home. I think memories can be revived if she could feel or see something that could trigger something from before. But what do I know, I ain't no doctor. I just hate to see her live like a pampered bird.

John was in his room with the music loud enough to barely be heard outside the door. He had his own part of the house, and I kept clear of it. I could call him, but it seems weird to call someone when you could just knock on the door. As he said, they don't bite. I made two taps on the door and I heard the music lower.

His footsteps tracked to the door as his shoes tapped against the floor. He swings the door open,

and a whiff of the air made it to my nostrils. I don't
know what he sprayed in his room, but the scent
was inviting. John said, "Hey, what's up? Everything
alright?"

"Ugh, yeah, I just had a question and wanted
your opinion."

"Yeah, of course. Did you want to come in or for
me to come downstairs?"

"It doesn't matter."

"You can come in." He moves back away from
the door jam, and I can see his room. It was neat not
only for a man, but for a woman too. He definitely
took after his mother. I came in and I didn't sit down
because I saw that he had a paint drop on the floor
and an easel set up. I knew better than to walk over
to sit uninvited. So I hung out near the door.

"You can come in and sit down. What's up?"

I took a seat at the nearest chair to the painting.
My eyes, I am sure, drifted to get a peek without
being too obvious. He didn't mention it at first, but
I could tell he saw me looking. He replies, "So, what
did you want to say?"

"Have you thought about–I don't mean to be
rude, and you can tell me it is none of my business.
But, is your mom allowed to go outside, go shopping,
or do anything?"

"I mean, we take trips from time to time, but we all chill at home for the most part. She likes being in her room the most, but she can of course go wherever she likes."

"So, if she wanted to go shopping with me or anything, she could come along?"

"Well, we haven't had her out in a minute. Sometimes, she can see people she thinks she knows. Sometimes it could be people who remember her. We thought it was safe for her to be home so we could watch her and make sure nothing happened to her."

"I get safety. I just think about whether staying in the house all day, if that really is a life a person should have to live if they were used to going out and doing things, is all. I am not a doctor, of course, and I trust you know what is best for your mother."

"I tell you what, maybe we can go for walks in the morning sometime in the future."

"Yeah, that works," I replied. Something was better than nothing.

"Okay, cool. Was there something else?" My eyes again thought I saw a piece of the painting. I was noisy, but I was wanting for him to set up the invitation. I couldn't hold my curiosity anymore, so I said, "I remember when we were walking up the stairs, you said you paint. Are you working on a new piece for the house?"

"It's just something for fun. I don't know what I am going to do with it."

"If you want someone to take a look and let you know what a regular person thinks, I would love to see it, or any of your art."

"Really, so you are into art, Fancy?"

I laughed and said, "I mean no, but I have a love for creativity. I am not all that skilled with stuff like that, but I like looking at good plates of food online when I'm scrolling. I wanted to be a head chef one day, but now, I am glad to have a break from the big restaurants."

"Okay, who's a favorite artist of yours in any field?" John asked.

"In music, Mary J Blige or somebody like that. I like old school 90s music. Don't laugh at me."

"You call that old school?"

"For us, anything before the 2000s is old. You can't be that much older than me." I knew he knew what I meant; he was just trying to be funny.

"Yeah, but I am sure I grew up differently than you."

"Why? Because you were rich?" I started to laugh a little bit and he replied to my kid with a dry laugh and said, "No, because I was sick."

"Oh, my bad." I felt stupid and insensitive. I should have remembered something more about him from what my mother told me, but it all went out the window.

"You don't have to apologize now for laughing at the sick kid. It's cool." He starts to joke around. "It ain't the first time people have laughed at me, and please don't tiptoe around me. We cool."

"I appreciate that. So what made you sick?"

"I had a lot of allergies. It was like everything made my skin bubble. If I had eggs, bananas, pine-apple, cheese, milk, or peanut butter–that almost killed me. I was just sensitive to so many things that I couldn't eat much of nothing, or at least it felt that way. My mom tried to make me feel good about it, but I hated it.

"She kept me away from anything that could trigger a response. I couldn't eat pizza, fries, several fruits, dairy products, and I only ate chicken, turkey, or fish. As a child, you just wanted some fishsticks, chicken nuggets, and fries. I never got that."

"I get dairy and stuff if you have allergies, but why not fried stuff?" I asked.

"I had a sensitivity to oils. I could only eat food from home, and no teacher dared feed me anything because they thought I would die. My mom embel-lished, in my opinion, how severe my allergies and disease were. All the school parties meant I ate alone or not at all. It was painful to see everyone having fun, eating, and joking, and I couldn't do it for a little while. Then I just accepted it."

"So you were sick with something else too?"

"Not exactly, with my rare condition of MCAS, or Mast Cell Activation Syndrome, everything had to be super clean. So this disease meant everything had to be clean, and I had to eat a strict diet. My mom loved your mom because my allergies were hardly there since we hired her."

"I guess that explains why she has worked with your family for so long," I replied when it clicked.

"Yeah, my mom kept me inside, and I lived through a bubble with very little exposure. My parents and brother made it difficult to make friends anyway. They shit became mine too often."

"Why, you say that? I mean, all brothers get in the way; they can't help it. You guys fight a lot or something?"

"Long story. But my life was different. Your mom was the best thing that happened to me. My mom thought there was nothing she wouldn't pay to keep me safe–with in reason. Your mom used to take me everywhere until I became a teenager. Then things got uncomfortable for us because I was becoming a man, and my mom stopped it all. We're not as close, but she is still very nice to me."

"Sounds like my mom. She has always loved children and especially boys. I had two brothers, and they could get away with murder, and she would find a way to make things okay."

"I envy you."

"We always envied you guys. You got every-thing–"

"It would look that way–" From the other room, Brittany calls out for her son. He leaves out of the room with Rain following behind him. She stops at the door as he enters. "Yeah, Mom?

"Where's your father? I thought he would have called me by now. His phone is going straight to voicemail."

"Oh, he might be caught up. I will give him a call."

"When you reach him, tell him I am looking for him. Is dinner already set for later? I was thinking to cook him something special tonight. Feels like I haven't seen him in years. I really do miss him, you know. When we were younger he would come home with flowers and make the whole house feel warm. It is so cold in this room."

"I can turn up the heat, Mom."

"No, Son. The heat I need is not a thermostat," she said jokingly and with longing.

"I don't want to hear anymore–"

"When are you going to bring your girlfriend around? You have been dating, haven't you?"

"Mom, I am busy with life and things. I don't have a lot of time for stuff like that."

"Well, get good grades, we're paying for that. Make us proud, but also enjoy your life. You don't live forever, and you don't get to choose when you leave here."

"You make sense, Mom. I will keep that in mind. Let me find Dad. I can send in Rain if you want to discuss dinner with her?"

"Yes, have her come in, thank you." He leaves out of the room while his mother sits at her vanity picking out earrings to wear. She had her hair in a stylish curl pattern as she looked over her makeup options. I came in the room, and she started to smile so big. I knew she really missed her husband, and it was hard to see her happy, knowing the evening she had planned in her mind wouldn't come.

I sat there and watched and listened to her make selections. She would think through the options and explain why one was preferred over the other. I could listen to this woman talk for hours because there was something delicate about her that made her intriguing. She was no weak person, and you can tell, but she would show moments that exposed her heart to you. She asked, "Okay, enough about food. How have you been?"

I looked a little like a deer in the headlights. She notices my hesitation and says, "I mean, you don't have family, a husband, children, or nothing? You are a pretty woman, so what's going on?"

"Oh, well. I have been busy with building on things with my mom. It's been a rough couple of years for us, so we thought to save up and go to Jamaica or something."

"That is a beautiful country. The mountains are breathtaking. I remember when Robert and I traveled there to Ochie. It is about forty-five minutes from Kingston. It is tranquil to see the water outside your window, lush and strong spring up outside your window. I rolled out of bed many times to be woken up by the sun. I miss the times when we could relax by the beach and bring things back for John."

"The pictures are captivating," I said, looking at her wall displaying the blue water and her and Robert smiling together in pictures.

"So are the people. The men are a bit flirtatious we almost got into three fights, and I am sure he slapped a few people outside my presence for their comments. Robert was discreet but no punk for sure."

"John didn't come with you guys?"

"No, he has extreme allergies, and we were con-

cerned about what medical attention he could need
that we couldn't provide there. He grew up protected, yes, I know. He might hate me for it, but I wanted
to make sure he grew up."

"Naw, he doesn't hate you and he does understand."

"What about dating?"

"I haven't found no one–"

"That part is good. I don't believe no woman
should go around looking for a man, but do her
thing, and he will find her."

"Yeah, my mom taught me that, too."

"Is your mom married?"

"No. She was married when we were young, but
that didn't work out. He got into drugs."

"Oh, sorry. I know that had to be hard for you
growing up?"

"It wasn't as hard as it could have been because
so many people in my neighborhood have the same
story."

"Hmmm."

"But, it was hard to miss out on events, though.
I always wanted to go to a father daughter dance. I

felt awkward to even bring it up to my mom because we had no one to fill in the gap. Then as I got older, my eldest brother started to take me."

"So you have a brother?"

"No, I had two brothers."

"Oh, okay, so your mom has three children?"

"Yeah."

"So, do they live with you or around town?"

"No, they both died."

"Oh, I'm sorry–I didn't remember you telling me that before. Did you tell me that already?"

"It's okay. They were both in the wrong place at the wrong time, I guess. They were always there for me when they were around, though."

"If you don't mind me asking, what were they like?"

"My eldest brother was kind, tall, athletic, and funny. He had a laugh that would make anyone around him start to laugh. He had a sense of humor that could be dark humor at times, but he could read people."

"My Robert is funny too."

"Yeah, my mom was big on keeping us inside before nighttime. She kept us away from everything, it seemed. But my brother would get involved in sports and things after school, which meant he could stay out later. She didn't like it, but she understood."

"Yeah, John didn't play many sports growing up. He likes to paint but did not like to play any sport."

"My brothers lived for sports and cars, especially my oldest brother. Eric was coming home one night after a game. It was far from the house, so taking a bus would have put him out really late. My mom wanted him home sooner than that, so reluctantly, she allowed him to ride with a friend home. A drunk driver who was high, hit them head on. Him, his friend, and the guy all died."

"Oh, I'm sorry to hear that, Fancy. I couldn't remember what happened to your family it has been so many years."

"Yeah, my younger brother Brian, he was a few years older than me, but he wanted to fill our older brother's shoes. We were about four years a part in age. It was like every time my mom thought to get her life together, her comes a guy making big promises he couldn't keep. They would stay for a year or two and leave when she got pregnant or life got hard."

"I know she got tired of starting over each time?"

"She did, that's why she is still single, and what makes me not in a hurry either to date. Not every man out here is a Robert, or a knight in shining armor."

"What happened to Brian?"

"He was on his way home during broad daylight. There was a drug deal gone wrong, and before he could take cover, they both started shooting. He was the only one who got hit. He died on the sidewalk outside our apartment complex. I ran down the stairs so fast because I saw him through the window walking."

I took a moment of silence as I felt the rush of anxiety mixed with anger rise up within me. "I didn't see who did it. I was not able to help my brother get justice, and my mom losing her second son broke her heart. They did everything right. They were not perfect, but they listened, never joined a gang, were good to people, went to church, but life still had a way of stealing them from us."

"Wow, I am really sad to hear about that. I can only imagine the pain your mother must have felt to lose her sons, but I know she is glad to have you."

"Oh, yes. We do everything together. I don't think I could ever leave her. She is my best friend, too."

"John is the same way. I am not sure if he has plans to die here. I don't want him too, but he can be so stubborn sometimes. Keep an eye on him for me?”

“Yeah, of course.”

“Let me know if he is dating someone. I want grandchildren.”

“You do? I thought you would be driven insane with small children running around this house with all the white you have.”

“I know how to make sure my stuff stays safe. I am not worried. Even if they broke things, I could replace it. People are not replaceable that mean something deep enough to you.”

I took a moment to take in what she said and replied. “I’d better get your lunch started. Also, what do you think about going for a walk sometimes in the morning?”

“Oh, I haven’t been outside in a little while. Maybe you are right. I love my window and the breeze that blows. Walking could be nice.”

“Yeah, you should get out. It is beautiful in here, but out there you could enjoy the sun on your skin, the breeze, the weather is perfect nowadays.”

“I guess I got used to staying in because John would complain when we went out. He said it was best he stayed in, so I stayed inside with him. I don’t want to be a burden to him, you know. He’s in school for art. He is so talented, and I know he would have a successful career when he finishes school."

"Yes, I see several of his pieces around the house and in his room."

She carries on and says, "I know one day he will leave me to live his life and I pray I have someone nice like you to help take care of me." Then she stops and says, "Wait a minute, did you say you saw his room?"

"Yes, but I mean no. I had a question for him, and he let me see some of his art. He is really private about some pieces."

"Yes, that is John. He doesn't want anyone to see what he is working on until it is finished. It's amazing how he starts a design to see the transformation."

"Yeah. Well, I need to go make you some lunch. So I will be back up."

"Sounds good. Let Robert know to come up when he arrives. He can be silly sometimes and fall asleep in front of the TV."

"Of course." I leave the room and head to the kitchen. I see John sitting on a barstool at the counter. He is on his phone, appearing to be deep in thought. I busy myself in the kitchen with my preparations, and as he finishes up his text conversation, he begins.

"I pray it is not too awkward for you to speak to my mom about Robert?"

"No, I know she loves him a lot and you. She asked me to remind him to come upstairs when he comes home."

He smiles. "Yeah. He would fall asleep in front of the tv all the time. The details are everything for her. So what are you making?"

"For lunch, I am going to make a salad with grilled chicken. Then for dinner, I was thinking to try this stuffed chicken recipe. I made it a few times, but never with vegan ingredients. I am sure of the flavors, but the texture is questionable."

"So you're experimenting on us?"

"No–but yeah. I like to experiment and try new things that challenge me. But why does your mom keep talking about you in school? Do you still go?"

"No, I took a break years ago when she got sick. Didn't seem right consider things."

"What? She thinks you will graduate, marry, and move away."

"No. I left school because I would find her down the street looking for our dad. She was a wanderer when she was first diagnosed. She couldn't remember her name. Left the house with less clothing than appropriate sometimes, and it just was a lot to worry about her and school. Then when things happened with my dad, school was out."

"I can understand that. She talks about you becoming a successful artist a lot. Is that why you don't tell her?"

"I try to keep things the same and hope she forgets the things that matter less, but she holds on to what she likes most about people. She doesn't remember the fights, the disagreements, or the bad times. It's strange."

"Did they tell you why she has dementia?"

"No one knows. I guess it is an act of God?"

"He works in mysterious ways for sure. My mom always told me He knows what is best. His ways are higher than ours. I learned to trust that even when things don't seem to make sense to me, he can make them workout."

"You believe in God?"

"Yeah. We have gone off and on when I was real young, but we became consistent when I was about twelve. My mom has been a faithful member at God's Greater Grace Church whenever she did go. It's funny because I was dedicated at that same church when I was a newborn."

"We grew up going to church here and there. Nothing consistent, though."

"What Christmas, Resurrection Sunday, and occasional Mother's Day?"

"Pretty much."

"I started doing that when my mom stopped going for a while. We started going back more years ago after my brother. You should go back. When life is hard and things don't make sense, I feel refilled when I go. When my brothers died, it was hard on our family and our Church family and God are how we made it."

"I will keep that in mind." His phone rings. He looks down at it and says to me, "Hey, I'mma head upstairs. Just call me when things are done, and I will come down to eat. You need a ride home?"

"No, I should be good. I am making both lunch and dinner now. If you are okay, I will head out after lunch."

"Yeah, of course."

"Did you need me for the weekend?"

"No, I should be good. My brother's coming this weekend, he always does for Classic weekend. So, unless I need you, I won't call. Try to go out and catch the Classics. It should be a wild weekend."

"Yeah, I am sure." He heads upstairs, and I continue to work. I hadn't been to a Classics since my brothers. They don't feel the same. I was never interested in cars. Funny how my mom would even let my brothers go with her trauma of vehicles. Eric loved cars, and he would remind us every year when the shows were happening.

It's been years since my mom and I went or even thought of the Classics. Today would be like any other night; we would be at home relaxing, watching tv, and laughing. I think sometimes if we should do something else instead. Are we wasting our time? Maybe I should read my Bible more?

I love God, but if I am honest, I don't read or pray as much as I should. I love church because it gives me a place to do it. Not sure if I go for the people or to know that I find time to fit in the things I should do at home. Talking about my relationship with God has always made me nervous because I fear what I would say if they ask me a hard question.

I always feel guilty when they speak about how believers don't tell others about their faith. Maybe I don't share because there is still so much I need to learn myself. I don't feel like a preacher. I know they say we are all supposed to do it, but my voice is not that great either, so singing in front of people has always made me uncomfortable.

But maybe that should change...we'll see. I do think that John was one of the first people I ever invited to church, so it might be hope for me yet.

CLASSIC
WEEKEND

Friday night was welcomed. It felt good to make a paycheck that required less of my time and was more fun. This is probably the first job to ever be rewarding and enjoyable, to pay and support a healthy work environment. I know things are early, but I pray this feeling and success stay the same.

Not sure if I want to leave now that I have met Mrs. Brittany. She makes talking and listening easy. I can see why we never moved, although I thought many times we should have. I think my mom regrets not moving after Eric died. Sometimes I think she blames herself for her son's dying. Their dads never showed up to the funerals.

I guess it was hard for them to place blame on anyone when they were never around. My youngest brother and his father I am sure she regretted that they weren't ever close. My mom is a faithful mother. No, she is not perfect, but she will always have a place in my heart that has no error. Her heart is pure, and she wants the best for us. I see that in Mrs. Brittany, too. I was in church yesterday, and they preached about Rahab.

Isn't it ironic that a prostitute was the great-grandmother of the Messiah? I wonder why we are so hard on people if the Bible talks about regular people like me who don't have it all together, being savable. Not sure if that is how you say that, but I do think like that.

I went into the kitchen as I gathered my thoughts for the day. I wanted to make something special for my mom. So I determined to make stuffed french toast, eggs, with bacon. She loves turkey bacon or turkey sausage. I am not sure if I ever had pork bacon; she was big on it not being healthy and being against her beliefs.

I never understood how bacon could be against someone's belief, but my mom was a strong believer in that. Turkey bacon is all I know, but working at the restaurant and smelling pork bacon, I'm not sure if I missed out. It crisped up differently than turkey bacon, so I wanted to try it, but then I wondered if I would get hooked and regret it. But you know the saying, you won't miss what you never had, and it's hard to unlearn what you have learned.

What I know, nothing beats the smell of cinnamon, vanilla, nutmeg, and freshly cooked bacon. I was eating with my nose as I soaked in the smells. I knew in moments my mom would hit the door with a face ready to eat. Sure enough, she came in with a smile and sat down. As we heard the motors in the background from cars driving down the street, we ate in nostalgia. Picking the moments that fit the occasion, and I swear I saw a single tear drop from my mother's eyes.

Days like this can be hard. I don't know what to say, so I don't say nothing. I sit in the atmosphere with her and just give her a hug or a nudge to let her know she is not alone. Sometimes, that is the best we can offer someone: our presence and empathy. I lost brothers, but she lost sons she bore and children she raised alone. I want so desperately to give something back to her for all she has done for us.

We eat, and she offers to clean up. Although I tell her it is not necessary, she says, "I will not clean everyone else's house and not clean my own. Go on." I leave out with a smile on my face and plop down on the couch. The phone "dings." It's a text from John. "Hey, were you going to the Classics?"

I text back, "Not likely. We don't really go to things like this."

"Ding." "So, what do you normally do?"

I replied, "Watch tv."

"Girl, you talk about my mom not having a life, I can't hear you when you volunteer to stay home every day. You gotta get out here and have fun. Let me take you."

Unsure of what to write. I look at the phone longer, "Ugh, not sure. I am with my mom."

"Ding." "She can come too."

I breathe out and slightly roll my eyes, remembering why I don't have friends. Days like this when I want to spend time at home, which is every day, they call and ask to go places. Prayerfully without regrets, I reply, "Okay, but let me ask my mom first. She is cleaning now."

He replies, "Okay, hit me back." I yell toward the kitchen, "Mom? You want to go to the Classics?"

"Girl, naw. I plan on sitting right here in the safety of my walls. Why?"

"John, Brittany's son, wants us to go with him to the Classics."

"You can go, but you need to be back early. I mean, like in a few hours. These streets get crazy at dark during the Classics. But I won't go."

I knew that answer before I asked. She will run from a car unless it is raining outside. She was unreasonable years ago, but she has calmed down some over the past few years. I was hoping she said no, so I would have a legitimate excuse. What do you say when you have a green light and you pray for a red?

I text back, "I have a few hours, but want to be home before it gets dark. I have some things to do for my mom."

"Ding." "Cool, I will be there in about 30 mins." Dang, that was quick. I was expecting to get an hour. Let me get my but up and get dressed before I talk myself out of going. Honestly, if I had more time, I would have come up with an excuse to not go. Just thinking this far has probably cost me a few minutes already.

I pick my norm, jeans, t-shirt, hat, and jacket. I don't know how the chill breeze finds me even on a day that looks like summer. I think I am anemic, and that causes me to be cold. Again, never diagnosed, just my hunch from my internet search and symptoms. Funny how in this diy society we can make anything make sense to us.

We don't have to have a medical degree to have an opinion, make a diagnosis, and determine a health plan. Ten minutes down, now what shoes to wear? Being lost in thought, people underestimate the time it takes to get dressed. I put my shoes on and look into the mirror. I look like a cute boy. I don't know why I dress like this sometimes.

I question is it healthy. "Ding." I check the phone, "Outside." I head out of the room and walk up behind my mother, sitting on the couch. Hugging her, I say, "He is here. I am going to go. You sure you don't want to come?"

"Yeah. You go and have some fun." She hugs me back and kisses me. "I love you."

I reply, "I love you, too, Mom."

Walking outside, there is Keisha staring and walking for the car like a fly to a light trap. She gets to the car, and I can hear her ask, "Hey, what's your name, and where are you taking my friend?"

"Name's John, and we are going to the Classics for a few."

"Her momma said she could go with you?"

I walk up behind her, "Yes, I am grown, remember. You are the one who has to stay in a child's place."

"Ain't you a church girl? You shouldn't be going out alone without a chaperon."

"It's not like that," I said.

"That's what they all say before they walk up pregnant."

"Ew, Keisha."

"Well, it's cool. You can come too if you want. We just hanging out," replied John.

"Okay." Without hesitation, she opens the door and gets in. I smirked as I hopped into the front seat. She just had to find a way. This girl swore she was grown. She doesn't waste any time before the questions start to roll. "So what do you do?"

"Keisha, stay out of that man's business. You ain't on no date or something. John, you don't have to answer that." He smiles, turns, and focuses on driving. I can feel Keisha's eyes zeroing in on my head. "Well, than whose car is this?"

"It's mine. Birthday gift."

"Wow, this is a nice first car," Keisha said while sizing him up.

"Yeah, I picked it. I really like cars," John replied.

"I didn't know you liked cars."

"Seems like you didn't ask enough questions." She smirks as he replies, "Naw, I don't talk about it much. I am not into them as deeply as some people, but I like nice cars and design. Kind of the creative aspects of car design, I guess."

"Yeah, I get that. I like Audi and Mercedes. I'm gonna have one, one day," chimes in Keisha.

"Yeah? They are nice cars." I raise a eyebrow listening to the conversation.

"What, Rain? You doubt me?"

"No, you seem ambitious and confident. That's good to make it at anything. I am sure you will find a way."

"I am trying to tell your girl not to worry about me, John. She swears I am a problem."

"She worries a lot?"

"I think so. I am surprised she is even going somewhere. She normally spends all her time in front of a tv."

"How I choose to spend my time is my business, Keisha," I say jokingly. "Yeah, it's no secret I love tv and I'm a homebody."

"Nothing wrong with that either," replies John. We continue to engage in small talk the rest of the way. We are all ready for a good time as we start seeing the cars. Like children in a candy store, we "ohh" and "aww" for the cars we like. John taps me and says, "Thank you." I reply back, unsure of what he is talking about, "For what?"

"My mom hasn't talked so much about anyone like she has for you this week. I wasn't sure what I could do to tell you thank you."

"Oh, it's no problem. I love your mom," I replied and said.

"She told me about your brothers."

"She remembered that?"

"Somehow, it's a miracle she did. Not sure how you have made it into her heart–and so quickly, but she likes you."

"I guess she really thinks I am Fancy?"

"Maybe, but thanks anyhow. Whatever you

want, get it. There is nothing I wouldn't do–within reason for you if you keep this up." I smile and we continue to enjoy the show. It was nice to have time away from the house and not to have to worry about money. I wondered if this was like being in Jamaica.

I know you can get everything included in your stay. Man, to live and not worry about money has to be a light feeling. I can't remember when I felt so light. It felt good. I said a silent prayer as we rode rides, "God, Father, if you can hear me. Please make this my reality. Show me what to do. In Jesus' name, Hallelujah."

I always wondered about prayer. Do they have to be long or short? Sometimes I fall asleep in church, and I feel so bad. We have one day a week to give to God and to fall asleep, I can see the problem logically. Praying for me should be easy and staying up, because I don't have long drunken nights or nothing that makes me have a reason to be sleepy. It must be the devil that sprinkles sleepy dust on my eyes.

I want the rush I feel on this ride for life. The excitement, the fun, and the laughs. If I am honest, I would rather be where I am than at home watching tv. The hours flew by, and I knew it was time for me to head home. I told John, "Hey, thanks for bringing me out. I really had fun, but I gotta get home."

"Yeah, of course. Let's get to the car." Keisha chimes in, "It's not even dark yet. Why we gotta go home?"

"I have something I gotta do. But we can hang out again. No problem." Keisha was smiling big the whole time, too. I think the way I felt on the inside, she felt on the outside. We all walked to the car with excitement and memories to last a lifetime. The trip home was filled with fun chatter, also.

We thanked him as we left the car and imagined he headed home. My mom had a few questions for me when I got home, and I had nothing but good things to say. "It was a great time. John is a sweet guy."

"Yeah, he was always a good child. Growing up, I loved spending time with him and seeing him grow up."

"He told me you two were really close when he was growing up."

"Yeah, I prayed over that baby every day. He was allergic to everything. I could barely come around him without fear of doing something wrong. He was a sensitive child, and his mother protected him like he was made out of glass."

"So how come he can do everything now?"

"Whatever he had going on, I saw the Lord work to pull it into control. I don't know if it went away completely, but he started to have more energy. He was sick less often. I watched a miracle in that young man's life."

"Does he know that prayers healed him?"

"Not so much. His mom didn't care what it was. She was just grateful. She and her family started coming to church a few times a year after that. So she knew something helped them, and I guess they did their best to thank God."

"What about Robert?"

"He was a smooth-talking man for sure. He was courteous to me. He never did anything sly or under-handed towards me. Very respectable, and I knew he loved his wife. I heard some things about him, and I know Brittany did too, but she didn't allow that to bother their relationship. She knew where he was living and putting his effort."

"So he became the hoe?" I jokingly said and started laughing.

"Don't talk like that, Rain." My laughter eased, and I read the room.

"Sorry, Mom. Bad joke. You right. She can't stop talking about him, though."

"She's been like that for years. He would come into the house, and she would be waiting for him. They had an affectionate marriage, and it was cute to see. If I could have been convinced to try marriage again, they would have convinced me. I loved the relationship I saw they had. It was heartbreaking to see him pass."

"How long ago did he die?"

"Maybe two years ago."

"When did she start losing her memory?"

"About three years ago. It was soon after Robert came home."

"Well, at least she has good memories to think about. It would be really sad if she didn't remember the heartfelt good stuff."

"Yeah. I think that was God's mercy." We kept talking into the late hours. It was a perfect day and night. I said my prayers before going to bed and thanked God for my mother and a good time. I felt grateful going to bed that night. Good thing, because the weekend wasn't over yet.

The Weekend...

I was home, and it was the afternoon. Kinda of strange, I was staring at a Bible out of the corner of my eye. I have seen the Bible this whole time on the table, but never once thought to pick it up. Today, something changed. I thought of reading it. When I got up to grab it, I heard "ding."

I picked up my phone which lit up, that sat by the Bible. Checking it, I saw that the text read from John, "Hey, I might need your help this weekend. I got a few things to do tonight, and I will need your help."

I text John back, "Of course, when did you want me to come?"

"I can be there in an hour to pick you up. I know this is last minute, sorry about that. I can pay you double for the weekend too."

Replying, I wrote, "It's all good. I will be ready." I put the phone down and picked up the Bible. I wasn't sure which page to turn to, so I just opened it and wherever it landed, I started to read. It was Psalm 91 in The Message Bible. I never could understand the other translations. I got this as a gift from a youth camp I went to at my church.

> You who sit down in the High God's presence,
>   spend the night in Shaddai's shadow,
> Say this: "GOD, you're my refuge.
>   I trust in you and I'm safe!"
> That's right—he rescues you from hidden traps,
>   shields you from deadly hazards.
> His huge outstretched arms protect you—
>   under them you're perfectly safe;
>   his arms fend off all harm.
> Fear nothing—not wild wolves in the night,
>   not flying arrows in the day,
> Not disease that prowls through the darkness,
>   not disaster that erupts at high noon.
> Even though others succumb all around,
>   drop like flies right and left,
>   no harm will even graze you.

I looked up at the clock, time was going, so I picked up my Bible and read as I walked to my room.

You'll stand untouched, watch it all from a dis-
tance,
    watch the wicked turn into corpses.
  Yes, because GOD's your refuge,
    the High God your very own home,
  Evil can't get close to you,
    harm can't get through the door.
  He ordered his angels
    to guard you wherever you go.
  If you stumble, they'll catch you;
    their job is to keep you from falling.
  You'll walk unharmed among lions and snakes,
    and kick young lions and serpents from the
path.

I put the Bible down on my bed and selected
the clothes I felt like wearing for the day. It was easy,
black. My hoodie did have "God Child" on the front
in white and pink. This was one of my favorite looks.
I was comfortable as I sat on my bed and finished the
psalm.

  "If you'll hold on to me for dear life," says GOD,
    "I'll get you out of any trouble.
  I'll give you the best of care
    if you'll only get to know and trust me.
  Call me and I'll answer, be at your side in bad
times;
    I'll rescue you, then throw you a party.
  I'll give you a long life,
    give you a long drink of salvation!"

I thought out loud as I finished the reading,
"Lord, I want a party! I don't know where I would

go, but if you could bring my mom and I to Jamaica, I think that would be a great time. We could use a vacation." I continued to converse with God in the open room.

It wasn't uncommon for me to talk to God like I talk to people who stand in front of me. I never got formal training on how to talk to Him. I just noticed that talking normally brought peace to my heart and gave me a sense of direction. What ain't broke I don't try to fix.

"Ding." My phone goes off again. John is downstairs, the text had read. I went to my mom's room and let her know that John was here to pick me up. She walked out with me to greet John and sent us on our way. I got in the car with Keisha looking on from her window.

I swear that girl is so nosy. She could be a secret eye or private detective with how much people watching she doesn't mind doing. I could never do it because I am too concerned with minding my own business. This is how you stay alive in the streets, my mom would often tell me. I listened most of the time unless someone I love I feel is in danger.

Why do we believe we are superheroes and can save anyone is beyond me. But that doesn't stop a broken clock from being right at least twice a day. Have you heard of such a thing? Old folk jokes sometimes get me. Anyway, we arrive at the house and things are dark inside.

John wasn't as talkative as he had been before. As we sat in the kitchen, I noticed he was worried about something, so I tried to spark a conversation a few times, but he kept looking at his phone. I asked him, "So, anything special happening today?"

"Well, I may have to go out today, but I don't know the time. I am waiting on something."

"Okay, I think I will be fine with your mom, so you can go whenever you need to."

"Yeah, I think you two would be good. I really do appreciate you coming on the weekend."

"It's all good. I am here to help. Did you eat yet?"

"Nah."

"Let me cook ya'll something maybe that will clear your mind. Anything you want?"

"Make it good, and I am good."

I heard the assignment, so I delivered. I wanted to make a skillet breakfast. I like how you can combine the items of breakfast, drop an egg on it, bake it, and boom, breakfast in a skillet.

Everything cooked up nicely and quickly. I brought a plate up to Mrs. Brittany, and she thanked me. She was still in bed, I guess she might not have been feeling all that well. I told her to try to eat and that might turn things around. I said a quick prayer over her in my heart and left the room.

Downstairs, I made John's plate and set it on the top counter. He looked up from his phone when he smelled the aroma rising from the plate. "You're not going to eat nothing?"

"I've already eaten. It's cool. The best time to eat breakfast for me is when it ain't breakfast." He nods and starts eating. The dim light that heaviness that was surrounding him was lifting. His hesitant smile had returned, and he grew more sociable with each bite.

"I know I am a little on edge. My brother is coming over and I try to limit how much damage he can cause. He and my mom don't get along and I put up with him because he is family. We don't choose them right?"

"I miss my brothers, but I do understand. Family can be hard to deal with sometimes."

"Tell me about it. So what about your friends? Do you hang out with them? Is Keisha a good friend of yours?"

"She is more like a baby sister. She doesn't listen. I keep a eye on her--with you around she has been more in my business lately. But yeah, I look out for her. Her life is kind of like mine. She had a brother too, but he was killed. I don't know the details, but he used to sell drugs, and their mother hated it. She warned him that would be the death of him when he started."

John didn't interrupt me as I talked. He just kept eating and listening. "He was still a kid, barely turned nineteen before he died. All the guys he ran the street with, not one of them showed up to the funeral. It's sad that the people some of us will risk our lives for, the same ones are not there when we need them most."

He scraped his plate clean as I finished the story. "They say his body was left behind a dumpster. No witnesses came forward. The investigation was an unsolved murder as far as we knew. I doubt they ever find who killed her brother."

"I hate stories like these. It really is sad."

"Yeah, what about you? Where are your friends from college or school?"

"We talk on the phone but I never really hung out like that. I am a homebody. I escape on the internet, but I don't do much."

"Do you play video games?"

"Sometimes."

"What do you play?" We kept talking games for a bit and decided to connect and play games in the living room. It was fun to hang out with him. Maybe this is what life feels like to have a close friend. I never had that growing up. My friends were usually at school or work, but we never hung out outside of work or school.

We played for hours, and I remembered I had to cook. He went upstairs to check on his mom, and I started looking in the pantry. I like the problem I had in this house. Finding out what I wanted to cook wasn't challenging because I wasn't missing ingredients. It was a conversation because I had so many choices.

Having the freedom to select my menu, ingredients, and pairings made me feel like a head chef. The problem I had with my old job, I didn't have here. Not one thing I have made so far has John or his mother not liked it. I was on a roll and wanted to keep it that way.

WHAT AM I INTO

As I busied myself in the kitchen, I didn't look behind me but I thought I heard John walk in. Before I could turn, I felt someone hit me and say, "What you doing at the stove, nucklehead?" I turned around and I was staring a stranger in the face. Taken by surprise, he stepped back and said, "Where's my brother at?"

"He's upstairs. I am Rain." I introduced myself after my heart stopped jumping. I see now why horror movies aren't for black people. I nearly died in this kitchen with no monster–or at least I thought there wasn't one.

"Oh, my bad. You the new cook?" He said as he took a step back to look me over.

"Yeah."

"I thought you were my brother. Ya'll almost the same height."

I couldn't tell if he was being serious or joking. I knew I wasn't his type, and I was relieved. I don't want anything to do with him, and he didn't like me either, so we are on the same page. I prayed it stayed that way.

But I don't know how he confused me with John. I think he just assumed, because of my clothes, I was him. We weren't really similar in height, and I wasn't his frame either. But I guess the baggy clothes could make me look bulkier than I really am. I dismissed the offense, and he left and went into the living room. I heard John come down a little bit later, and he said, "Aaa, I thought you were coming later tonight?"

"I had some time. Just wanted to check on you, dame. I don't get a warm greeting? A hug or some-thing?"James says as he goes to plop down on the couch.

"My bad, Bro." He extends his hand to dap him up, but James doesn't budge he just starts smiling and says, "You can do some of the corniest shit. Just say what up." John shrugs it off and goes back to his phone.

"Whatever, hey," he says as he starts scrolling nonchalantly.

"See, that's what's starting the rumors in the street. Why don't you boss up sometimes and get mad or something?"

"You know I don't care what nobody thinks about me. They pay they money, like or ignore me, we cool. That's what a jar-head like you is for if we have a problem, right?"

"Reputation is everything, though, John. What people don't fear, they don't respect."

"Yeah? Was that something you learned or dad told you?"

"I am the reason we are where we are. People fear me, and they better respect me." James flexes as he sits on the couch. You really couldn't tell him that he didn't single-handedly raise the family out of the clutches of poverty. This family appeared to be financially stable, but he wouldn't let anyone say they helped more or equal to him. John ignores James, and he replies, "See that's what I mean. You gotta loosen up. You look tight."

"I don't need your social advice, James."

"Now I see why you single. So what's up with the cook? She your type? The boy-girl type?"

"Man, nah she works for us. She cool, so leave her alone. Mom really likes her."

"She ain't my type, you already know that. I like em with thick legs, fat ass, and big titties. She ain't got none of that."

"After the last one we had to fire, it will never happen again."

"So you still blaming me for that?"

"You were sleeping with her, and her boyfriend came up here to fight. He thought it was me."

"Yeah, I don't know how he got us mixed up. We ain't nothing alike," said James in a snotty, macho way. John looked up and stared him straight in the face and replied, "You didn't have the gun in your face."

"I had a few guns in my face, but none of them lived to tell the tale."

"I ain't like you, James."

"That's why this family needs me."

"You think that?"

"Why would it not be true?"

"You are messy, James. Things don't have to go sideways all the time."

"So, you were the one who pulled this family out when we almost lost everything? When you were at school, working on being Picasso, I was out here doing what I had to do."

"Here we go again." John looks back down at his phone.

"Ya'll got a funny way of saying thank you."

"Whatever good you do, you overstep the limit,

and death comes. If only you had restraint." James is growing impatient with John's dismissive behavior. He starts to raise his voice as he says, "So what are we talking about?"

"I ain't saying nothing. What have I said?"

"You just keep sitting your bitch-ass over there. You could have done something, but you didn't. I swear this family got selective memory. You think you're the only one that had dreams taken from you, John? I might be a jar-head to you, but I ain't no dummy. I understand strategy on a level you don't know."

"I didn't say that you didn't, James."

"But you sitting over there like you don't do shit wrong. You got a past like the rest of us. You think because I don't tell nobody, that I don't know?"

"What? Know what, James?"

"The real reason you single."

"Come on, James. You believe that, too? You know dang well the truth. You were there."

"I know you gay, John."

"I already told you, I'm not gay. I didn't do anything that would make me gay."

"Really?"

"Yes, really. Not everyone is going to act like you. We different people."

"Dame right. Ain't no way, I would let another man get close enough to look like he wanted to kiss me before I chop him down."

"James, whatever. You be imagining things."

"I saw you when you were with the neighbor. Nobody else gotta see it, but I did."

"What you think you saw, you didn't see. It wasn't like that."

"So he didn't lean in and kiss you?"

"Come on, James. I ain't dealing with this to-night. I ain't gay. I didn't kiss him, and I don't owe you an explanation for what you saw."

"Did you ever tell Dad?"

"How could I? He hardly talked to me before he went to prison, and when he got out, you got him killed. Remember that?"

"There you go. I bring up your little gay thing, and you want to talk about me killing Dad. You can blame me for Dad, but I didn't kill him, and we both know it. You just hate facing the fact that you ain't no saint either. We both have an ugly past and lifestyle that could send us to hell. You've got flaws like the rest of us. Skeletons are in your closet, too so remember that as you try to play the Carlton card. Ain't nothing hidden with me. I'm a man about everything I do and stand ten toes down."

"So, that makes you better than me? That makes you feel good that you are the wild Fresh Prince of where? This ain't Bel-Air, but you swear that it is. You grew up sheltered, too. Sleeping with however many women doesn't make you no man, either."

"No, my results make me better than you. Having sex is normal, and I got a strong drive with no complaints."

The friendly conversation was growing dark. I wasn't sure of what to do as I worked in the kitchen, but in earshot of the commotion. I slid my headphones on and readied my smart watch to play anything loud enough when the voices started getting closer.

They didn't cool off, but it appeared to be safe for now. I kept working as the voices escalated. I knew it wasn't much I could do with a brother's quarrel, but stay out of it. Next, I heard John say, "You really think you are better than me? Why? Because you will sleep with any woman walking? Because you can wave a gun around?" He continues, "You will never understand me, and I stopped expecting you to."

"No, because I know what to do and how to handle business. I am not scared and hanging on momma's titty. You need to grow up and take action. You still live at home and you are nearly thirty, what kind of sad shit is that. Grow up!"

"Is taking action what you were doing when Dad got shot?" Replied John.

"That's the bullshit I knew you were gonna do. I was doing what I had to do. Dad made that choice, not me. I never asked him to do shit for me. When he was in prison, I was the one who visited him. I was the one who did what he and Mom told me to do. I was the one who had to be the monster so this family could survive, and you give me your ass to kiss. Fuck that. Fuck you John."

James takes a swing at John, but he ducks, and James misses him. I heard him stumble over a side table or piece of furniture, and then I shuffled closer. The next swing in the living room had to be John's because I heard it land, "pop."

James must have charged John because large pieces of furniture must have moved with the friction of the legs scraping across the floor, based on the sound I heard next. Moments later, I heard Brittany coming down the stairs. I wanted her to get out of her room, but this isn't the way I thought it would happen. She comes down yelling, "Get away from my son!"

She has a baseball bat in hand and she is squaring up, looking at James. She looked at him and didn't flinch. She wasn't the sweet, shy lady who is happy-go-lucky that I know from upstairs. She was strong, fierce, and she stared at him with icy eyes.

She said, "If you don't back the hell up, I will beat you down with this bat." I was like a fly attracted to the light as drama encircled the room. I was peeking and making sure I didn't knock over anything.

James says, "You don't know who I am? Mom, for real? You don't know your oldest son?"

"I know you are in my house."

"So I am the one you blank out of your memory? You've got to be kidding me. You the worst villain in this house, and you get to act like a saint, too? This is some real bullshit. You can't be for real."

" I don't know what you and John got going on, but this is my house and you ain't gonna be tearing up my furniture with your shit. John, you need to get your friend."

"Mom, for real? You don't know who I am? After all the shit I did for you? You don't really remember all the shit you had me do? You don't remember all the stuff you made me do or I had to do to protect John?"

"John, I told you. You ain't gay. This better not be some secret you holding out from me. Who is he?" She looks straight at John without a smile.

"I ain't gay. Get the fuck out of here. I am your real son, James. We have the same parents. You and Robert."

"No, the hell you are not. I would remember if I had another son. Now get the hell out of my house before I call my husband!"

"I live here too. This is my house too! I am the reason we still got this shit. I pay the bills. Not this sorry shit, you call your Son."

"Watch how you talk about him. If my husband heard you, he would beat your ass down to the ground. You gonna regret raising your voice."

"Your husband? Your husband is dead and has been dead for years. He ain't coming back!"

She swings the bat, "You watch how you talking in my house. Like I said, you got one more time to take another step, and it will take the police to calm me down. Is that what you want?" She swung a few more times, and James started shuffling around the room to get away from her. He might be bad on the streets, but up in here, his momma is still Queen.

John speaks up, "Mom, put the bat down, please. He was just talking shit. He shouldn't have said that. Let's breathe and go call Dad." She looks at him and tries to calm her eyes and lower her wrist. If she was honest, the weight of the bat was more than she lifted in months. She was showing signs of being tired after swinging it a few times.

"Naw, ain't nobody coming up in here doing shit." She replied. "This is my house."

I called from the kitchen in a calm manner as if I was on a different planet, "Hey John, the food is ready." I had to keep my voice calm because I wasn't sure how this night was going to end. I prayed it would end with me leaving out the door and soon. John replies, "Yeah, Rain. Thanks. Make another plate for James."

"He ain't staying here. This mother–" John now holding the bat was able to gently hold his mom. He was moving her toward the stairs and says, "Mom, it's cool. We just was–"

"I don't have to stay here for this shit." James interrupts.

"Look, go get something to eat. We got something to do later anyway. I will take Mom upstairs." John says as their mom looks down still trying to gather her bearings. The burst of energy was coming down now that she was reflecting on everything.

Brittany looks up to John and says, "I don't think it's a good idea, John he stays here." John looks at his mom and says, "Do you trust me. We were just playing. We like brothers, and we do this sometimes."

She snaps back with a bit more fight, "He better not be the reason I don't have grandchildren."

"Trust me, the boy-girl in the kitchen is closer

to being his type than me." Brittany was about to snatch the bat back, and John snatched it away in time. "He's just talking, Mom. We good." She is a bit unsteady going up the stairs. The surge of energy with her not already feeling well, made her light-headed.

I put out the plates, and John insisted on taking Brittany her plate. She was still worked up, and he was concerned about her, I could tell. She hadn't heard for months that Robert was dead. Whenever she found out he had passed, it took her time to bounce back and get happy again. James sat at the table. He made some colorful comments about the food being good. He didn't say much else.

I wasn't sure of what I should do, so I changed the music on my headphones and started to clean up. I didn't have much of an appetite and I couldn't wait for John to come down the stairs. He came into the kitchen, and James said, "She good?"

"Yeah, just tired. She didn't feel well today. But she's alright."

"I'm bought to head out. I can just see you at the club later?" James said.

"Yeah, no problem."

James gets up from the table and walks out. John sits at the table with his food in silence for a little while. "Did you hear any of that?" I sat at the table, "Naw, I had my headphones on." He looks at me, "I had them off for a little bit, but then I put them on."

"My brother is a ticking time bomb. He brings hell wherever he goes."

"I see what you mean. So you two not close at all?"

"We never were close. We are different, and I guess, he was my dad's favorite and I was my mom's. I don't think they loved us any less, but we just pulled to one parent over the other."

"So that's why your mom doesn't recognize him?"

"That and probably because he is a asshole she hoped to forget. But I really don't know. My mom, our mom, wasn't the easiest to grow up with. I had it different than James. I was sick, so she was more patient and loving toward me. I get why James is angry, but he needs to be accountable for his mistakes, too."

"You said he's the reason your dad is dead."

"You had your headphones off for a long time."

"Sorry. You don't have to answer if you don't want to."

"Naw, it's cool. My dad sold drugs. I am sure you knew that." I nodded my head in agreement. "Well, he got charged, went to prison for like ten years, then he got out. My brother and I were seventeen and fifteen. My brother had to become the man of the house, and whatever my dad left unfinished, he had to finish."

"My mom protected me, so I never got involved with whatever that was. I was in school and focusing on my grades. I knew getting to college and moving away was what I needed to get away from everything. But life moved fast. My brother dropped out, but his grades were never really good anyway."

John took a drink from his cup, "I think he hated all of us for what he had to become to keep things going. My mom knew what she had to do, but she needed someone she could trust to be her eyes and ears. I was in and out of hospitals sometimes, so she never replaced my dad either. It was all on James."

"Dang."

"But when our dad got out, he came home. Things were different about him. He wasn't the same man I remembered growing up. He would sprawl with me to tell me I had to become a man. But I was eleven or twelve. How was I supposed to be a man like that?"

John's Flashback...

"John, put your hands up." His dad, Robert, replied.

"I don't want to do this, Dad."

"Son, you gotta learn. Painting and all that is great, but you gotta become a man. You can't be focusing on that stuff so much, you don't develop."

"Dad, I ain't cut out for this."

"To become a man, John? This is not an option."

"I am just not a fighter. I don't think that means I won't be a man, Dad."

"Really, so if a man comes and tries to steal your wife. What you gonna do about it?"

"Dad, I am not old enough to have a wife."

"This the stuff I am saying to your Mom. She and Connie are making you weak. From now on, ain't no more girls' trips. You going grocery shopping, or any of that. You are going to learn what it takes to become a man, because that is what you are, a man."

"Dad–"

"John, I said what I said. You need to grow up." His phone starts to go off. "Now you practice by yourself. I gotta go, but we will pick this up later."

Back to Present…

"My dad and I were never eye to eye. James was more like him, but he lacked the finesse. My dad came back from prison a different man. He wasn't as aggressive about molding me. He was grateful to have anything, and it was like each moment he loved it. And I get it. Being locked up, not able to think or decide things for yourself, is a mind jerk; and I am sure he missed us."

I got up to get myself a glass of water. "I am still listening. Just a little thirsty." As I saw the food in the skillet, I made myself a small plate. I didn't realize how hungry I was and would likely get seconds.

"Yeah, so my dad didn't want to deal with drugs or anything like the past. James thought he would have someone to identify with, but he didn't understand our father anymore. Robert tried to get him to change his life, but he wasn't having it."

James' Flashback...

James and Robert were in the living room in a heated situation. James was passing and Robert was using his hands to speak louder than his words. "Son, what are you doing?" Robert said to James as his eyes were wide opened and jaw tight.

"What do you mean? I am making sure everyone knows who we are. Do you not remember what happens when we lose our grip, Dad? Weren't you the one who told me that when the fear is gone, the respect goes also? So what the hell are you talking about now?" James says with veins popping in his throat.

Robert tries to gently grab James by the shoulder, but he shakes away, "James, I know this is hard to understand. I didn't understand it when it started to happen to me. It is a process I went through, and I am believing that God will change our lives for the better."

He walks up swiftly in his father's direction and snaps back, "That's your solution, Dad? God? Just exactly where does He fit into the shit we created? Does he support selling drugs, Dad? Will he approve killing people, sex, alcohol, and clubs?"

Robert, aware of the escalation and the sound of his words, tenderly replies. "No, no, of course not."

James refuses to take his foot off the gas of emotions stirring within his belly and replies, "So what the hell am I supposed to do? I don't know if you or Mom recognize this or not, but I cannot just walk away. If I go hugging trees like you, or lose my mind like Mom, where does that put this family exactly? In a shit hole somewhere, I can tell you."

"It doesn't have to be that way. We can get jobs and reinvent ourselves. We can afford to take care of your mom off investments. We can get our stuff together and make a life, James. I don't want for you what I got. I want you and John to be better than me."

"I already am. I'm not dead yet or in jail, so I have been doing some things right. Don't worry, you and mom can retire and I will do this shit on my own. I was doing it while you were locked up, so what difference does it make? Just stay out of my way."

James tries to move past his father, but he stands in his way. "And if I don't?"

"You might get rolled the fuck over."

"Wow, so that's how you talk to your father now?"

"You haven't been a father to me, Dad, for the past 10 years. The streets raised me, and it always has. When you were out, you gave me this life, you instilled principles that built me for this. I don't know what the hell you are on, and it is not helping. But I shouldn't have expected anything different. I was stupid to think things would be different for me. I am alone, Dad. None of you get me, no matter what I do, I don't measure up to what you, Mom, or John expect. So the hell with all of ya'll."

James pushes past his father, bumping into him as he walks. His father stands there for a second, a bit dazed by the conversation. The last few months have been stressful and hard on both of them. Robert didn't know how to connect the dots he had formed away from his family.

They had no idea how much he had been praying not only for himself but for his entire family while away. Although he was not physically around them, he became a Believer in the power of the Word of God. He knew he didn't have to be in the

120

same room as them for his family to benefit from his prayers. Like the Centurion who asked Yashua to heal his child who remained at home, he believed God would do that for him, too.

He saw an enraged James walk out the door, but he refused to walk out of his life. He couldn't give up on the family; he was partly to blame for their failure and struggle. He wept bitterly, realizing the pain he caused and how much more he needed Yah, God Almighty, to save his house.

Back to day...

John clears his throat and says, "James and my dad struggled the years he was back at home. My mom losing her memory during the last year of his life was hard on us all. I gotta admit, him knowing God was better than the version I grew up with. I remember some of the conversations we had together."

"What, what did you talk about?"

"He told me he was proud of me and he loved me. He saw how I had taken care of my mother and his wife, then he thanked me. I didn't need his thanks though, I did it for me. I love my mom, so I did it for her."

"Did you ever hear that growing up?"

"Not once. I thought I was a total failure to my father. At first, when he said it, I didn't believe him. I thought he was playing mind games or something.

But that day when I heard him and James fighting, I knew he was genuine."

"What about your mom? How did she respond to the new Robert?"

"She loved him more. Robert could do no wrong in her eyes. She loved my father every day of his life. She would wait up for him nightly to return home, and it was their thing to speak each night about their day. The phone bill for him being in prison was pricey. James paid for it and never complained."

"I am sure that was hard for him?"

"Yeah, me too. But what does he expect us to do? I think he wants something that no one can give him."

"Maybe God is what he needs. When you try everything you can, and that doesn't work, it might be time to try God."

"Look, Rain, I am not big into religion. I mean, I will say thank you, God, or pray when I am in trouble like anyone, but I don't believe in God like that."

"I used to be like that, too. When my brother died, I didn't want to believe in God anymore. I kept replaying my pain, and it was turning me bitter for life and everybody. I am still healing in a way, but I learned that hating God got me nowhere. It made my problems compound, and I was drowning."

"So what did God do to make you feel better? He didn't bring your brothers back."

"No, but he loved me through my loss. He showed me how to honor my brothers. He reminds me of the good times. God really helped me see my mom needed me, and I needed her to survive. I wasn't alone, although I felt that way. I didn't want fear and pain to be an everyday thing anymore. I chose to let things go especially for what I couldn't control."

There was a bang at the door that caused me to jump. John looked at me and said, "Put your headphones on and don't take them off."

EVENTFUL
RIDE HOME

I might have a nosy streak in me, but today I was keeping the blinders on. As I shuffled around in the kitchen, I was sure not to be too loud as I loaded the dishwasher. I didn't want to be too soft or too hard. I think either one could make me look guilty of something, though I wasn't sure of what.

I heard feet stomping across the door frame. It sounded like more than just James came back to the house. There was another guy or a few, I couldn't tell. I could hear the quick feet of John rushing to the door and slamming it shut.

Whoever was there was trying to talk, but when he would try, it sounded like he got punched or something because his voice would muffle out. John replies, "What are you doing here? You know, Mom would kill you bringing this stuff around the house. We live in a white neighborhood."

"You think I wanted to do this? I couldn't bring him to the club. It was cops everywhere," replies James. "I had no choice but to bring him here."

"What's going on?" Asks John.

The guy who was likely dragged there by James tried to speak again, but this time I heard the thump. The guy was saying, "Listen, James, it's not what you–"

James interjects, "Don't say another lie to me, man. I hate liars. My mom taught me that one."

"Look, I know it looks bad, James, but I am telling you. I got set up. This is all bull–" He must have gotten hit again. His words were cut off mid-sentence. James' voice carried when he said, "Do I look like a fool to you? You think I am stupid, don't you?"

"No, no, I don't think you stupid. This is why I can clear it all up."

James inquires further, "So, how exactly are you going to do that?"

"I can show you the guy who set us both up."

"Why do you think you are here and not him? I know what Courtney was gonna do, the only person who got set up was you. You tried to catch me but I am too smart for that shit. You bet on the wrong guy, and I pray whatever they sold you was good enough."

"Hold up, James. We not about to do that here."

James asks, "What time is it?"

"Man, I don't know, it's late." I looked at my watch, it was about 10:00pm. I heard the guy start begging, so whatever was about to happen, I sure prayed it wasn't what I thought it would be. The guy started pleading, "Come on, man. This is not the way things should be, James. I was set up, I am telling you. If you just give me a chance, I can fix it."

"Shit like this don't get fixed, it gets dealt with. I don't need snitches or bitches around me. If you going down, you go down. We look out for anybody down with us. My dad did a dime for this game, you think you supposed to be different? What makes you special? We would have had you, your girl, and your kids. What did you get--and don't lie?"

"I didn't get nothing," replied the crying man.

"That's a dame shame." And just like that, I heard a muffled, "Pop-pop!'" and a thud. The room grew silent. James said nothing, and neither did John. I was frozen still for a moment, and I was praying not to do something stupid to break the silence. I don't know if it was me or that God betrayed me, but in that moment, I dropped a fork.

I quickly turned up my headphones and the intensity was erased by the pumping music blasting in my ears. I didn't hear nothing as I moved calmly, trying desperately to control my shaking. I was rattled, but I couldn't show anything.

I think I heard a faint conversation of James asking John, "What the hell was that?"

"It's Rain, she's still here cleaning up the kitchen."

"I thought she left hours ago?"

"Naw, we were talking for a bit, and then she started cleaning. She should be done soon."

"So you think she didn't hear any of this shit?"

"Man, she is autistic. She wears headphones that blank out everything. She don't know nothing."

"You better pray that's the case."

Have you ever felt like someone was coming through a door, but you didn't know when? You wasn't sure where to stand, how to look, because any look felt guilty. Out of reaction, I turned my back towards the kitchen entrance. I assumed he would walk that way, and I did the only thing that made sense: I opened the fridge and put the leftovers inside.

When I closed the door, there was James. I was startled and I jumped, "Oh! Dang, James. You scared the crap out of me."

"Did I?" He said inquisitively. I didn't break a sweat with my responses because my momma told me a bear can smell fear. So I had to be calm as a cucumber. "I didn't know you were here. I was just finishing up."

"How long you've been here?"

"All day. John asked me to come over, and we hung out after I worked for your mom. Did he leave?" I didn't want him to think I was here just in a domestic capacity. I did play the angle that we could be more than friends, not sure that I sold it. But I didn't want to look like the help. I've seen enough movies to know the replaceable people can disappear quickly, too.

"Right," he starts to smirk. "So you got a thing for my baby brother, don't you?"

I start to grin slightly as I smirk and say, "Yeah. I think he's cool, I mean." As I pull back my excitement trying to look genuine. "I was hoping he could ride me home and we could talk."

"He had some other things to do, so he stepped out. Do you always have them things blasting like that?"

"Since I was young, I had them. I think I am autistic, but my mom never had me diagnosed. I need the music to help keep my world in focus, you know?" He nodded his head, but not looking clear about what I meant.

"It means I have a slight delay when it comes to society, people, talking, and stuff. I don't talk about it much, and please don't tell John. I didn't mention that."

"It's cool. I got you. So, how much you got left to do?"

"Not much, just cleaning the stove. I put the dishes in the dishwasher, cleaned the pots, and put the leftovers in the fridge. You can eat if you were hungry, I made enough."

"Thanks. You go ahead and finish." I finished cleaning up why he looked on at what I was doing. I wasn't sure if he bought it all, but I put it on as thick as possible. Lord, forgive me for using the autistic line, but I slick do think I could be. I just don't know. So is it a lie if I don't know for sure that it is a lie?"

After abandoning the thought, I put my coat on, and James said, "Hold tight. I can take you home."

"You sure? I mean, John normally takes me, or I take the bus."

"You don't have to be scared, I don't bite. I will let John know I took you home." We walked out the back together, and I knew I couldn't look back. I couldn't look like a sheep going to the slaughter, or I would be treated like one. I acted as if everything was cool and nothing had happened. I got into his car, and I was quiet as he drove.

"You don't talk much, do you?" James asked to break the silence.

"I do, but it's usually about video games or talking to my mom. I am home a lot, so I play games, cook, of course, and watch tv with her. I am my mother's daughter."

"Yeah, your mom is cool. She's worked for my family for a long time. She practically raised my brother."

"She told me that she and John were close." After a few minutes of silence, I asked, "So, what was John like, I mean growing up? He said he was sick a lot."

"Yeah, he was like the kid that should have been placed in a balloon. He couldn't do shit. Going outside, it was like the air made him sick. I never seen nothing like whatever the hell he had going on with his body."

"So it was that bad?"

"Yeah, it was worst before your mom came. I tried to play with him and he would get winded like he had asthma. His body seemed to overreact to everything. We never had that brother rivalry that guys need, I guess."

"Yeah...I don't have any sisters. I was the only girl in my family."

"Oh, how was that?"

"Great at first. I loved having older brothers. They would try to be like a father figure to me, which always made me want to laugh, but their hearts were in the right place."

"I don't have a sister. My mom thought John

was a girl for the longest. My dad would say, 'That ain't no boy in your stomach. That's a little man." They joked about it until he was born, and my dad was right. All the little girl stuff she bought had to be taken back to the store. I wonder if that played on his mind growing up?"

"Why would that mean anything?"

"Nothing, just thinking."

"I live right over there." I pointed to my complex, and he pulled up to the curb to let me out. I couldn't move fast enough to get out of the car in my mind, but my motions were normal–or at least I thought so. I told him, "Thanks so much for the lift, and please don't tell John about the autistic thing. I know it can weird people out." He nodded his head with a slight smile, and I got out and shut the door behind me.

I walked to the front, and I kept my eyes straight long enough to feel his gaze shift from me. I didn't hear the tires move away from the curb, so I wondered what had taken his attention. I didn't turn around then, but I kept walking until I got into my building. When I was a safe distance away, I peered out the window.

The distraction was none other than Keisha. She was leaning on his window like a hooker in a 1970s movie. I don't know how she put on that short dress so fast; it was like she was Superwoman and went into a phone booth to come out like that in a flash.

She was talking, and I thought James was going to drive away and leave her standing there.

He didn't. I saw her fast tail jump in the car, and the two of them drove down the street. I quickly came out of the house and started walking. I wanted to know where they were going. I didn't know what to do. I called John and I asked him. "Hey John?"

"Yeah?" His voice sounded uneasy. He didn't speak casually like normal, he was more reserved. "Do you know where your brother might be going right now?"

He said rather sternly, "You asking for my brother, Rain?"

"No, it's not like that. My neighbor's daughter went with him. She is underage, and I thought he should know."

"Oh, I told you Rain–"

"I know what you said, but this girl don't listen. I just need to find her so her mom doesn't kill me."

"Okay, he probably went to the club not too far from your house."

"Okay, thanks."

"Hold up, maybe I should go with you?"

"You are far away. I will get there before you do.

I can meet you there."

"Alright. I will be there soon as I can. But don't walk up to him. He becomes another person in there."

"Got it, I will keep my distance." We hung up the phone, and I didn't know what I would do. I prayed it wouldn't be a dumb move that cut the leash shorter I had already tightened. I walked up the street that I had tried to avoid all these years. The night scene changes everything in this neighborhood. It never looks great, but it looks a whole lot worse and scarier at night.

I walked past a guy who I couldn't tell if he was hungry or strung out more. If there ever were a zombie apocalypse, I am sure it would look like the night-scape of tonight. Dark, overcast, with people walking from random places. Walking at awkward speeds of fast and slow, with no clear direction of where to go. I couldn't walk fast enough.

I reached the door and showed my ID. They looked at it twice and I prayed they did the same thing for Keisha. If so, she is sitting in the back of the club or walking home already. I went inside, and as I looked across the room. A handful of people were there, and the music was blasting. The dance floor was empty, and a few groups were sprinkled around. I guess it was too early for the crowd. It didn't take long to spot her and James sitting in the VIP section.

I thought to walk over there to clear the air and

walk her tail up out of there, but I saw a big dude step in my way. I replied, "Hey, I was just here to come and get my sister." He leaned down and said, "I don't give a dame who your sister is, you ain't getting past this line."

"No, I am just trying to tell you and the guy she is with, she is a minor. She's not supposed to be here."

"I don't know what you are talking about. I really don't care. My job is to guard this section, and so I cannot let you pass here."

"But I need to–"

"Look, if you don't move on, I'm gonna put you out." I could hear it in his tone, his eyes didn't break to have a glimpse of empathy as I talked to him. I knew he was serious about kicking me out and making a scene. I couldn't do that, and maybe this was God's way of keeping me far away from James. I said another quick prayer to thank God for saving my life as I went to sit near the door.

I sat there and watched her laughing and talking to James like she was twenty-one. She was drinking and smoking, and neither one looked like her first time. I knew them girls she hung around were trouble, and now I am seeing just how much. I couldn't help but look around and feel the sticky feeling closing in around me.

The music was nothing like what I listened to. I

don't know who was rap-singing at the moment, but neither one was he doing well. I don't know if the dj was paid or what, but I did see James motion to change the song too. It was that bad.

I thought it felt like thirty minutes before I saw John come through the door. He pulled me off to the side and said, "Did he see you?"

"No, the bodyguard blocked me."

"Alright, just hang tight, and I will take you home. Don't come near the section though, I don't want no problems."

"Of course." He walked away, and I was relieved to see him. I knew he would get this sorted, and I would be home in about ten minutes, good timing to watch something I missed on tv. I binge-watch shows, so when I am working, I sleep as much as I can, so on my off days, I can get it in.

I saw him go to the same troll who told me I couldn't pass the bridge, and he let him by. John walked up to James, who didn't stand but he gestured to him. Keisha smiled at John, but it wasn't a friendly welcome. I would say it was a "I told you so" look. I didn't like seeing it, and I think John was a little taken aback by it, too. With the music so loud, I could only guess how the situation was going.

He didn't sit down, and James made no motion to permit it. They talked for a few minutes away from Keisha, and James looked back at her. I think

John must have told him her age. He looked back at John and said something. Not sure of what, and John said a few other things.

Looking at the conversation made me wonder how anyone liked reading movies with subtitles. I tried to get into K-Dramas, but I couldn't do all of the subtitles. I like to hear actors and people talk. It was equally weird to watch a B-Drama in real life with no audio. The body language was jumping off the screen when James swiped his arms in a dismissive way toward John.

He sat back down by Keisha, and she snuggled up against him. He put his arm around her neck, and John walked out. I think he was coming in my direction, but I didn't see Keisha following him. I stepped closer to the door in hopes we were living, and maybe she would be walking out after us. The two of us walked into the night and I had to ask for the dialogue to match the communication I just saw.

So I asked, "So what happened? She coming?"

"Naw, she ain't coming."

"What you mean? You told him she was under age right?"

"Yeah," he says it in a nonchalant way.

"So, that's it?"

"What am I supposed to do, Rain? Snatch her

up and make her leave? She wanted to stay. I know
she heard what I said, and she didn't say she wanted to go home when he asked her if she wanted to
leave."

"Wait, so what do you think is going to happen
to her?"

"I don't know. He could smash or he might not."

"You think the two of them will have sex, John?"

"I don't get into my brother's business. But he
sleeps with a lot of women, Rain. He is not looking
for love. Your friend might just be another one. I told
you to stay away from him."

"I did, there was never a worry for me. But–"

"Look, we need to get out of here. Let me get
you home."

I walked to the car with my head down, and
John didn't try to linger. We got into the car and
drove in silence for a while. I thanked him for the
ride, and I sat in the car for a few more seconds
before he said, "Look. I am sorry about your friend.
I have seen it a million times. He uses women, Rain.
Try to talk to your friend, but I ain't sure she's gonna
listen."

I knew he was right. I saw her body language
that night. She liked where she was, the security,
the lights, the sticky air, and wearing sleazy clothes.

It was who she wanted to be no matter how much I wanted that to change; it was the choice she was making. I couldn't accept it, but I did wonder if she would force me to.

I knew better than to ask questions I didn't want the answers to or to wait around for questions I wanted to avoid. Before he could speak up about something else, I said, "I am going to go upstairs and lie down. I am drained, and I think I'm just going to go to bed."

"Yeah, of course, but hit me up in the morning and let me know you good."

I got out the car and said, "Yeah, I will call you."

I didn't plan on calling him. Man, I was lying like crazy today, or was I? I was thinking and speaking before I could think. Was I lying or really just sleepy, half crazy, or scared? I still hadn't processed what I could have heard and I don't know that I want to revisit it. I couldn't think of one person to talk to because my mom knew them, too.

It was an awkward place to be in, deciding on if you will say a word or keep quiet. Technically, I saw nothing, so what could I do about what I heard? I am not even sure what that was. I was a jumbled-up mess, and I couldn't put all the pieces together. I really did need to sleep, so I guess I didn't lie.

Maybe this is the most honest I have been about how I feel in a long time. Could this be part of God's plan to make everything work to my good? I always wondered about that verse. How can everything work to anyone's good?

Surely somethings have to be for the worst. What about Keisha? Could this be for her good? Why do people–teenage girls have to be so hard-headed?

I know she could see what I did about James. Why would she choose to be with a viper? She is barely legal, and she is already trying to pull somebody. I am approaching my mid twenties, and I couldn't care less.

Are my priorities out of whack? I am really thinking of sleeping now because my feet began to feel like weights as I got closer to the door. Putting the key in the lock felt like labor, too. If my mom didn't know better, she would have thought I was the reason I came home late.

When I entered the house, she was sitting there waiting for me. She asked, "Where have you been?"

"Nowhere, Momma. I was just looking for Keisha."

"She ran off with that guy, huhn?"

"How do you know?"

"I got ears everywhere. Sister Pat saw her and called me when you left."

"I am sorry to wake you, Mom."

"It's okay. I couldn't sleep until I knew you were home. It's just what moms do."

"I am so tired. It has been a long day."

"Like an ice cream before you go to bed long day?"

"Yes, that kind of day. Maybe even a glass of hot tea after an ice cream kind of day."

"Okay, yeah. I will join you." My mom and I sat at the table laughing about our shows. I prayed she didn't ask about work, because I honestly didn't know what to tell her. I couldn't lie to her, and I knew she would see through it anyway. My momma, like most black mommas got a built-in lie detector that be working. Between them and God, all your business is in the streets.

I was glad for the time and how she was able to calm my nerves. I don't know how I looked to everyone else, but inside of me I was spinning on a merry-go-round looking up at the sky, seeing the room spin. I haven't been drunk, and I don't see it happening. I hate the taste of alcohol. One of my brothers dared me and I tried it. It tastes like the green alcohol stuff in a bottle with a little sugar, nasty and strong.

My mom never has to worry about me with that. I am good. The tea was so welcomed. I love chamomile and lemon grass tea when I can't sleep. I don't think I will struggle tonight to sleep as tired as I am. But after drinking the tea, my eyes could barely keep open, but my body had trouble resting. I kept thinking about Keisha and her mom.

I knew she was up waiting for her like mine. It broke my heart to see how hard her mom worked to provide for them on her own, to see the disrespect she gets in return sucks. Keisha doesn't listen to her mom, respect her, or even pretend to like her. She only complains about what she wants, and if you ask me, she is selfish.

Not sure if you call her a narcissist or not, but she doesn't appear to care about anyone but herself. I know that can't be good. Not sure how God will swing this to be good, but I believe He will. I prayed that He would.

I think I stayed up for about two hours, then drifted to sleep off and on. It must have been four in the morning before I heard a door slam that woke me up. I was a light sleeper when I was on a mission. Tonight I was on a mission that a pin drop could send me into high alert. I heard her voice, although I didn't know what she said. She swished away, and I saw him looking.

"Nasty." I don't see how some men just don't care about stuff like this. How could they be so heartless? I pray that I never find out. I saw her enter her building, and I knew her mom would take care of it from there. The light was turned on, and I knew the match would soon begin. Either the next day, she would have a black eye or something, or she would be grounded.

Either way, that meant James wouldn't be around for a while if she didn't want to blow her image. My heavy eyes were begging to return to sleep. It was like a light burning on my eyelids as I quickly drifted back to sleep. I must have curled up with my pillow and started snoring because I had drool all over my pillow in the morning.

It was one of those nasty I am so tired, don't care about my own image kind of sleeps. I mean, I was dead to the world, and I thank God when I awoke to rub the crusty bits off my cheek. Just thinking of it made me shake my own head too, but a girl's gotta do, what she gotta do!

I looked at my phone and I thought, should I call John? I didn't call him, but I sent him a text letting him know I would call him later. I was still honestly tired, but I didn't want him to worry about me. He clearly has a lot to deal with being family to James. I lay in my bed debating on if I should get up, brush my teeth, wash my face, and then cook. Or, lie here until I fall back asleep. My undecided mind chose to lie there.

I heard "ding" on my phone. I checked it and it was a thumbs up on my message. He liked it something we hadn't done yet. He normally replies. Not sure what was up.

HEEDING THE WARNING

Getting up early on Monday morning I was debating on what to do. Do I call out? Do I call in and say I will be out, or just not show up? Which would be less damaging, and as far as I know, safe.

I looked at my phone and saw a text, "Call me," from John so I picked up the phone. I guess option two it is. "Hey John, I got your text."

"Yeah, I wanted to let you know I will pick you up this morning if that is okay?"

"Uh, well, actually I was going to–"

"I know you were going to ride the bus. Don't worry, it's cool. I will see you in about an hour." He hangs up and doesn't give me a chance to respond. Not sure what that was about either, but I knew it was something I would ask about later. I got up feeling tired.

I don't know why I felt so drained and under-motivated to get started with the day. Not sure if it was the swarm of thoughts, questions, and serious concerns floating around my head or something else.

Had my mother ever dealt with something like this I wondered. I didn't want to ask, because I didn't want the answer or for her to feel she needed to answer. Either way, it seemed dangerous.

I had only one direction at the moment: go forward. I took some time that morning to pray harder than I had in a while. I needed that Psalms 91 kind of coverage working with this family. I thought to read something else from the Bible, although I was unsure of where to turn.

I did the infamous go-to, opened the book, and where it landed, I started to read. Psalms 23:

"The Lord is my shepherd; I shall not want.

2   He makes me lie down in green pastures.
He leads me beside still waters.

3   He restores my soul.
He leads me in paths of righteousness
    for his name's sake.

4   Even though I walk through the valley of the shadow of death, I will fear no evil, for you are
    with me; your rod and your staff, they comfort me.

5   You prepare a table before me in the presence of my enemies; you anoint my head with oil;
    my cup overflows.

6   Surely goodness and mercy shall follow me

all the days of my life,
and I shall dwell in the house of the Lord Forever."

Not sure of how I should feel after reading this, but I didn't feel as much fear as I had before. I knew this was for me right now, and I intended to believe that so I could face what could be around the corner. Walking out, I had hoped to see Keisha around. Normally, she should be out to catch the bus for school, but knowing her fast tail, she was sleeping, planning to come to school later.

I prayed I was wrong, but if I was right, I would catch her later this evening, I hoped. She really needs to pick her friends better, I'm telling you. Breakfast was simple, I didn't have much of an appetite. Today was perfect for a bowl of cereal before I left for work. I got outside and a few moments later, John pulls up with a half smile.

I get in the car, trying to be as relaxed as possible. I know we are both on edge and soon we will have to break the silence. He turns the music lower and says, "So, how are you?"

"Honestly, a bit shaken up. But I am good. It's a lot going through my mind, is all."

"I know it is, and I am sorry. I wanted to talk to you yesterday, but it wasn't the right time. I know that."

"Yeah, it's whatever–"

"Before you say anything, let me explain. I know you don't want to work for us anymore, and I can't say I blame you. But I know that James is on to you, and I can't have anything happen to you. Do you understand what I am saying?"

"I think so." I replied, a little relieved but also nervous. I know that God got me though as I walk through the valley of death, so I won't fear no evil.

"I knew you probably didn't want to come in today, too. I can't blame you. But if you quit now, I cannot say how the next few days will go. If you can do my an honest favor and stay with us at least a couple of more months, I will make sure you are good. I like you, Rain, and I couldn't live with myself if something happened to you."

"Well, dang...Thank you. I don't know what's going on, and I really don't want to know. I pray you and your brother know what you are doing."

"I know this is scary, but the house I live in on the outside looks like a castle but on the inside, it is more like Beast's sanctuary. This is normal and I am not proud of it. Being around you made me forget about the dark side to our lives. I really wanted James to be on his best behavior but he keeps finding a way to screw shit–I mean mess things up. Sorry."

"It's cool. Thanks. We can't control our family, but you need to be careful, John. I don't know what to tell you to do, but I know to tell you to be careful."

"I appreciate that. I don't know what you told James about us, but I want you to know we have to keep it up. I don't want him thinking we are screwing with his mind. Let's just say he doesn't like it... So, you want to go shopping?"

"Yeah, that's cool. I need a few things for the house. Thanks!" We drive for a bit in silence. It wasn't an eerie silence but one that settles the atmosphere and is a comfortable silence. I knew where things stood and what I had to do for now. I was grateful for God using anyone he wanted to cover me.

We pulled up to the mall, and I was a little confused. I asked, "I thought we were going shopping?"

"We are. Let's go shopping!" He said with an honest grin. This man is full of surprises, I tell you. I don't know what it was, the wind, or something that washed over me, but I was calm and even happy. We walked together into the mall, and he grabbed me by my hand. I was a little shocked, but it was something I needed. I needed to know that I wasn't alone and he proved he was here with me.

We walked into the mall, and the scent smelled like the mall. It was light in the air, and I felt like I was walking on clouds for a second. He looked at me and said, "So, where do you want to go?"

"I can't tell you the last time I was in a mall. I have no idea."

Then he looked at me and said, "Then we can walk until you find somewhere you want to go." We started at the door and enjoyed small talk as I saw each store begging for attention and customers. Some stores had associates standing at the door to welcome you in and others to keep you out. I have seen the fashion brands on tv and on social media, but being in the mall, the stores didn't make me want to walk inside.

I preferred the down-to-earth stores that looked like locals owned the shop. We casually walked in, and I saw a few things that caught my eye. As a painter, John must have been taking good notes of my facial gestures because he started to speak to an associate. Another lady walked up to me and asked, "What's your size?"

I replied, "Oh, size 6." With only one word, she said, "Thanks," turned around, and walked off. I shrugged my shoulders and kept window shop-ping in the store. I wasn't planning on asking for anything. I was just happy to get away from my thoughts. I thought to gather up the things I liked in my head and get the top three things.

However, when I turned around, I had two asso-ciates holding clothes draped over their arms. "Miss, we grabbed these things for you to try. They are all a size 6. We guessed your shoe size, you look like a size 7."

"Yes, I am a seven." I replied, shocked.

"Great. Follow me." I followed behind them with a puzzled gesture sent in John's direction. I went into the dressing room and it was spacious. They fit all the clothes I picked with my eyes on the racks and he yelled to me, "Okay, let's see what you got." One outfit at a time, I tried them all on. I got more excited with each fashion change.

John was loving it and I was puzzled on why. I thought most men hated going to stores and shopping like this. I would show him a fit, and he would give me a nod when it looked right and a thumbs down if it failed. He was a pretty good dresser, and I was glad. If it was up to me, I would have picked jeans and sweaters, of course in black.

I liked the clothes on the walls, but I didn't picture me wearing them. I liked them for other people. It felt like a hour went by and I was still trying on things he had added to my quick finds. I realized the stuff I liked most weren't the things I picked, but the things he suggested. I had two racks of clothes going, the ones that I wanted to keep and the others I planned to put back.

From the rack I wanted to keep, I had a divide between the things I really wanted and the things I really liked. I wasn't thinking to get it all. But! John told the associate to ring it all up. I almost dropped my jaw at the sight of the bill. I couldn't do anything but smile and whisper thanks to God. I don't know how this day happened, but I was grateful.

This wasn't the only store we had this M.O.

(mode of operation) for, we did the same thing in like five stores. We went to shoe stores, a dress store, a computer store, and he even got me a new phone! I was beyond words and insisted he take some things back. He laughed and said, "Please. Don't make me feel poor. I don't like the feeling. You good."

I laughed at him and we enjoyed lunch and talking in the food court before heading home. He had ordered something for his mom. Surprisingly enough, James made sure it got upstairs to her. Today was the day off I needed, but I did not expect it to go like this. I didn't have all my worries behind me, but some of the immediate ones were gone, for sure.

He drove me home and offered to walk me up. Normally, I would have declined the offer, but with all the bags, I couldn't say no. I was praying that not too many people were looking at me. Around here, you don't want to be too happy about anything, it makes you a robbery target. We "snuck" the bags into the house with a less flashy bag, a trash bag! Hahah, I was paranoid for sure, but John understood.

I did have a great time, and he thanked me for allowing him to escape his circus, too. He left and I couldn't stop thinking about the day. My mom came in and saw the three trash bags in the living room and said. "Girl, what is going on? Did you stockpile trash?"

"No, Mom. John took me shopping." I replied.

She replied jokingly, "Where? In the dump?"

"No, the real bags are inside the bags. I got you a few things."

"Me?" She said, and I affirmed she heard me correctly. I gave her a fashion show in our living room, and she loved it. We enjoyed our time together, and I cooked while she watched her show. I looked out the window, and I saw Keisha coming in from wherever she was. Didn't look like school.

I checked the time and it was later than school hours, so I wanted to find a moment to get away. I stepped out of my apartment in an attempt to catch her before she entered her unit. "Hey, Keisha. You got a minute?" She turned around and gave me the "What do you want face."

"What's up, Rain?" She said with a " I don't have time for you" tone.

"Look, I just want to warn you. I saw you last night, and I don't think you should be running around with grown men you don't know, especially if you don't know their story."

"I don't need another mom, Rain. But if this is your way of looking out for me, thanks. But I know what I am doing."

"Really?" You think running around with grown men and hanging out at clubs is what you should be doing?"

"So you saw me last night? I knew it had to be you. Look, stay out of my business, Rain. You blocked me from John, cool. But you cannot stop me from James. Besides, you probably wished you had the bigger fish."

"Girl, this is not about being in competition with you. I am an adult, and I can live however I want to. You are a child, just because you have boobs and attitude that doesn't make you grown, Keisha."

"I don't need you looking out for me. I never asked you to be in my business. If you have nothing going on in your world, please don't make me your real-life drama. I don't need saving, and I am not a damsel in distress. I am doing what I told you I would, making a way for me."

"I just pray you know what you are doing. Not everyone out here has the best hopes for you. You are a baby and you think you know, but you have no idea of what's out here."

"I am not a baby, Rain. I am a woman, and yes, I might be young, but a woman nonetheless. I will have a better life than this. If I have to work my way out or claw my way, I am getting out of this dump, Rain. Look, I am sorry, but you will have to under-stand. I am not that little girl across the hall any-more. You don't have to worry about me."

She opened her door and disappeared. She could never know how much I was invested in her life. I remember when she first moved here, and her mom was dating her father. He was a lowlife, I mean a guy who had no high hopes and only wanted to bring others down around him.

I remember one day coming home and seeing her outside on the front step. She was downstairs, scared, I could tell, but she said nothing. I sat next to her and just kept her company. I knew things were rough for her, but I didn't ask questions. Sometimes asking makes things worse. So we sat there until my mom got home, and I told her.

She told me that the next time things got heated, I should let Keisha come to our house and keep her there until she got home. I did that, and that's why she is more like a baby sister than a neighbor to me. It always stings when people turn their backs on you, especially those who you know will need you for the road ahead.

I didn't know the future, but I knew it wasn't heading in the right direction. What do you do when the people you want to help won't listen to you? You see the wall and know that they don't, but they are too hard-headed or headstrong to hear you.

I could keep trying, but I knew she had made up her mind. She was her mother's daughter but also her father's, too. She had both of them plus her own mind, and I had to let her make her own decisions. But I will warn her mother and see what she can do.

I can't tell her much because that's dangerous. Maybe I could encourage a curfew or something? I had to think on how to say it without saying much, and for the time being, I may have to do nothing. I know her mom knows she is out here, but just not by how much. How can I show her without making things worse?

I needed to think, but I certainly didn't want Keisha to ruin a good night for me. I saw her tiptoe out again that night, but alerting her mom would only make her worry more. I didn't see a way to have a win with this. So I prayed for the best solution and left it in God's hands.

I went to sleep that night after that prayer and slept.

Months later...

Over the next few months, I really struggled seeing her leave nightly, going to do only God knows what. We had a few conversations in the hallway, but she didn't say anything much different than before. Now I see how some old heads feel when I sometimes think the same way. We all can think we know what we need when we know what we want.

John and I grew close, and we became equally invested in each other's lives. Thank goodness James didn't come around the house much. Selfishly, I was glad Keisha kept him busy, and whatever else was going on. Things seemed to be going well for everyone.

I went to the house one day and John called me

up after lunch to his room. He said, "I know you have been wanting to see this. It wasn't done when you asked and I get nervous when people ask–don't know really why, but I do." I smile sheepishly and say, "It's cool. I get it. It's an artist thing."

"That's partly why." He lifts the curtain and that's when I seen it. It was something I didn't think I would see, me! Not just me in a cute and romantic or fun way, but one of the most embarrassing photos of me. It was a painted replica of my face and appearance when I fell onto the couch wearing the heels I could barely walk in. He cemented the moment, and I could do nothing but laugh at first seeing it.

"John, are you serious? You put a curtain over a drawing of me falling, and then had the nerve to paint it?" After laughing for a bit more, I said, "I thought you saw me when you were giggling, but I didn't think you would draw me?"

He went along with the light air, thank God he wasn't offended by my laugh, and said, "Sorry. I just couldn't get you out of my head. The moment kept replaying in my mind, and next thing I knew, I was drawing. Something I haven't told you, I haven't drawn anything for a few months, almost a year. I was uninspired."

"You mean to tell me this moment made you pick up a paintbrush?" I said jokingly.

"Yeah, pretty much. I hadn't thought about why painting made me happy in a long time. A lot of things have changed over the years. With my dad's passing, I drew a lot of him."

"Really, I didn't see any of his portraits." He walked over to a cabinet that was closed. He opened the door and began to show me drawings. He had several that depicted the type of father he had. He drew endearing photos, but many that seemed disapproving. He almost drew him as a monster in some. So I asked, "How were things with your father before he came back?"

"They were terrible when I was younger. He thought I was never manly enough. No matter what I did, how I dressed, talked, or walked, it always needed to be tweaked by him. He was so critical of me growing up that the only time I didn't live with anxiety was when I was with your mom. She just let me be a kid."

"I am sorry you had to go through that. I know my mom got a lot of looks from people at church and stuff for how I dress, too. It's not that I don't like dresses and girly stuff, I just never had a reason to wear it. It's like when I do, people applaud me like I was lost before the dress."

I continued to say, "I know what it is like to be judged by others and feel like they have missed seeing you because they struggle with accepting your differences from their reality. I used to try and please people and do things to make others judge me less. That didn't work either. I didn't want my life to be like that. No one has to deal with me 24-7 but me, so

I gotta not only like, but learn to love myself."

"That makes sense. I get to be me with you, and you are like one of the best things in my life now. I pray that doesn't make you feel no kind of way." I shook my head no, and he said, "I wished I grew up with someone like you. I don't know why your mom didn't bring you guys over much. Your brothers came over a few times. I think your oldest brother knew James?"

"I am not sure. My mom doesn't mention them much. We used to do a lot of stuff for their birthdays, but now I think she is focused on healing and not trying to resurrect the dead in a sense. And I am proud of her; this year was the first that she didn't really cry a whole lot."

"If my mom knew each day that my father died, I could only imagine her tears."

"Have you ever told her about what really happened?"

"I did once. She was hysterical. I mean, throwing things, cursing, and saying what she would do if she found out who did it. She was really scaring me. She would go from this calm lady, you know, to the mother I had."

"Wait, you mean your mom wasn't like this growing up?"

"No. The woman you know, I had no idea she

existed. Don't get me wrong, I knew my mom loved me and at least accepted me, but she didn't believe I was fit for this family, either. She wanted to shelter me and provide me with a way out. She honestly tried to send me to school and get me a clean slate, but my father wasn't having it."

He kept talking as he sat down on the couch next to me. "He would tell her that he had two sons, and both of them would be strong men. He was big on legacy and building an empire for the family. He said it took all of us. My mom really bought into that, too."

John's Flashback...

Robert and Brittany are sitting on their bed. Robert had just come home from a long day of being out and Brittany was dealing with school issues for John. She wanted to talk to Robert about them, but knew how he felt. She tried to be soft about her approach, but knew the outcome might be the same.

"Robert, I need to talk to you about something."

"Yeah, what's up?"

"I was thinking about something the teachers said about John. They say he is really gifted and could do well in math courses and maybe be a architect or something. What do you think about putting him in a program over the summer?"

"You know how I feel about this stuff. I don't

mind him building whatever he wants, but this family has a future, Britt. We gotta be ready, and there are things I wanted to give to the boys."

"What if he isn't really meant for this like us. I mean, he is really smart and could do well corporately."

He says jokingly, "So you saying I'm dumb, babe?"

"No, but you know John isn't like us."

"We had this conversation before. He is part of this family, and if I gotta make a man out of him, I will. But I won't have him embarrassing me or this family. We are the Jones family. I have worked to get here, and I won't let anyone take that from me, from us. Yes, John is whatever, but he will be fine. He just has to find his way and I will help him. Okay?" He gives her a kiss, and she smiles and says, "Okay."

The two of them get lost in their love for each other, and a young John leaves the outside of the bedroom door. He heard the day his life was sealed by his father to be a life of crime, and it pained him to know he had no choice for what direction his life would take. He was mad at God for giving him this family because why should his father be the only one to pick his fate?

He tried over the next few months to win his father over with his talent, skills, and showed him his test scores. All he dismissed. He kept putting him in different sports. Tackle combat sports, he was the worst, but his father wanted him to learn to fight because he said every man needs to be able to defend their family.

He left the boxing gym many nights with bruises and black eyes. The school would call, and the family would say it was from the gym and they had the proof. Nobody could see his abuse, his pain, or his shame. He left every meeting in physical and emotional pain. He couldn't rely on anyone to save him, not even God.

Modern day…

"So your parents didn't see eye-to-eye on how to help you?"

"No, my parents agreed on everything as far as we could see. My dad had the final say on everything, and I knew it. I knew after that conversation my life was as good as sold. I would amount to whatever my father picked, and he did that when he wasn't the man he became. I wished I had the father he tried to be to me before he died."

"How was he different–if you don't mind me asking?"

"Naw, I don't. He would encourage me at things. He would tell me he loved me and was proud of me…I thought he was full of–crap because he never said that to me when it mattered. You know?"

"Did you ever forgive him?"

"I tried to, I really did. But I didn't trust him. My dad wasn't a sneaky type, but he was never mushy and loving to anyone but Mom. I cannot say that I ever even saw my dad cry."

"Never?"

"Nope. Not at funerals or anything. I was crying and he would tell me, "Choke that shit up. Men don't cry, Son. I had to hide my feelings from my dad for all my life. And then, when he wanted me to forget about all of that and accept this new soft or human-dad, I didn't know what to do. It could have been a test, or a game he was playing that I didn't know."

"What makes you say that?"

"I remember once he told me that I could tell him anything. At first, I was hesitant, but he kept saying it. Kept asking, "Is there anything you need to get off your chest?"

John's Flashback...

"Dad, naw, I am good. I am just dealing with my shit." John stops talking and his dad continued to stare at him with inquisitive eyes knowing that there was more. He asked the question again wanting for John to open up and speak to him.

"Son, if there is something you need to talk

about, I am here to listen. If you got questions about
life, school, girls, or other stuff, I am here. Look, I
know I am busy, and I told your mom I was going to
do better at being here for you. So if you need me.
Here I am!"

For a moment, John thought he could believe
him. He took a deep breath and asked, "What if you
realized you got feelings for someone and you don't
know if they think about you?"

"Okay, so you got a girl you like?" His dad nods
his head, "You are young, so a lot of what you feel
is probably puppy love. Nothing series. If they don't
like you back, no big deal. Move on. There are plenty
of girls out here. You will find one or a few you like."

I hesitated, but I was quiet long enough, and
he said. "Look don't tell me this gay shit James was
saying is true? Come on, Son, we can't do that in this
family. That just ain't right. You know we ain't religious or nothing, but that will get you sent straight
to hell."

"But what if I was born this way?"

"Is that what that boy told you? You were born
this way? You weren't born no kind of way. You are
my son. I am your father. He can listen to whatever
his parents tell him about his life, but you live here.
Here, ain't no gay. You are not gay. I am not gay, and
I didn't bring no gay sons into this world. Sure, you
different, but that don't make you gay."

"I don't think I am, but–"

"So you liked that he kissed you?"

"No–it's just, I mean–but no he didn't–"

"Look, just stop this shit. I can't take this. This just ain't right. And I, and I know God ain't punishing me and let my son be gay." Robert motioned with his hands and got up to walk away. John came to try and say something to him, but his dad turned around and said, "Look, ain't no son of mine gay or thinking about being gay. If that shit is on your mind, you need to erase it. I ain't raising no gay son."

Back to today...

"He didn't want to listen to me. He wanted me to say what he expected. When I didn't, he turned his back on me. This wasn't the only time; it was many times like this. Anything I tried to be real with him about for how I felt, or about what I was thinking and dealing with, if it wasn't his way, he would say it was wrong."

"There was no conversation, no debate, no nothing. Just his way. So I learned to keep my feelings and thoughts to myself. He would ask stuff, and I said what I knew he wanted. I gave him peace about his life, no matter what it was, but I had none."

I gave him a hug. I didn't look at his face too often when he was talking. I wanted him to get it all out. As I hugged him, I didn't say anything, I just

held on to him, and whatever he wanted to say,
he said. That moment was between us, and that is
where I intended it to stay. I wanted to be the safe
place for him to speak and share whatever he wanted.

PUMP THE BREAKS

The months seemed to fly by. The last few months were quiet. I was trying out recipes, and the friendship between John and me was strong. We would hang out on my days off and just be ourselves without the pressures of life. I wore the dresses he bought me, and we went to dinners just to see what a date would feel like.

We were both rusty, and we pointed it out. If I were to date someone, I realized how much I wouldn't have mind them being like John. He was a sweet guy and I thought he was manly enough, even though I knew he battled on believing it for himself. We talked about his father often, but I just started praying for him, because a lot of what I said, I realized, didn't change his heart.

Sadly, I wasn't sure if he still didn't blame God for how his life turned out. He would make comments that made me think he still wanted God to do something, or wave a wand and reverse time. I know God can redeem time, but nothing about him reversing it.

One time we were eating, and as we were

talking, I noticed Keisha across the way. At first, I didn't say anything; I assumed she would be here with James. I didn't see him, but some other guy sitting at the table. I prayed for her sake that she wasn't something serious for James. I figured he had a lot of girls, but still, some dudes feel some kind of way when they are treated like meat.

I knew she needed another sisterly talk on one of my trips to the bathroom. I pulled her aside and said, "Girl, what are you doing?"

"Here we go. Why are you here? And are you in a dress?" Keisha looks down at my outfit, impressed.

"Keisha, focus. You can't be out here with him. This isn't good for you."

"We are just talking, Rain. I am not with him. We ain't sleeping together if that is what you are thinking."

"It doesn't matter. It looks wrong, Keisha. Tell me you know this?"

"I am just talking. Ain't nothing wrong with that."

"You are really stupid. If you out here with James, and now you out here with him, regardless of if you're serious or not, it looks wrong. You need to leave and go home now!"

She gets closer to my face and says, "Stop butt-ing your nose where it doesn't belong. Go try and get some dick or something. Maybe that will help you relax. I don't need you trying to be my mom or big sister. Whatever this is, stop it. I told you, I know how to look out for me."

I stepped back in her face and said, "I know you are smelling yourself and thinking you are a boss chick now, but you are in dangerous waters. If you only knew how small you are in this circle, you would be more mindful of where you step. You are ruining your life before you had a chance to live it."

"No, Rain. I am living my life, and you just can't stand to see it. I don't need you telling me what to do."

"Fine, you want to play these adult games and gamble with your life, I pray you know what to do if you crap out."

"I do. Go with a bigger fish." She grabs her bag and walks out of the bathroom. She sits back at the table, and I know John saw her this time. I tried. I knew it was going to be bad now. I went back to the table and sat down. He asked the obvious questions, "Was that Keisha?"

Reluctantly, I said, "Yeah."

John asks, "She came here with him?"

"Yeah, she said it was nothing serious."

"Everything is serious. If I were you, I would tell your friend to leave town tonight. News like this travels fast–very fast. I won't be able to do anything, Rain."

I knew what he meant. So we got our food to go. I didn't want to make another scene at the restaurant so I looked up a bus trip on my phone and thought to do what he said. Get her out of town at least for the next few nights. I didn't want to tell her mom, I knew that would drive her crazy but I was thinking what was best for her life.

If she knew where she was, maybe she would go to her, or worse, she would be made to talk. I prayed it wouldn't go to any of this. I was scared, but I had to think fast, and that was what I was doing. I leaned on my energy to keep me calm. We waited outside for her to come, but she didn't come out for a while.

John told me, "Go home, Rain, and let me wait around for her."

"You sure? I don't mind waiting with you." I replied.

"No, you go home." His breathing made me get out of the car. I knew better than to argue with him. I trusted him, but I didn't trust James or the other dude she was with. She came out of the restaurant laughing and smiling. She was fine. I was going to go home as I waited on my ride, but as she got into the car, I saw a third person in the backseat pop up like a jack-in-the-box.

Who was that? The brake lights came on, and the two of them drove out of the parking lot. My driver pulled up, and I asked him. "Can you follow that car up there. Stay a few cars back, though."

"Hey, I gotta follow the trip."

"I will tip you $50 if you just stay on the car."

"No problem. Is your boyfriend in the car?"

"My Sister."

"Yeah, I would do the same thing."

As we followed the cars, I knew where she was going, to James' club. John was not too far behind the car. I guess he saw what I did, but he didn't tail behind. I had the driver pass the club and drop me off around the corner. I gave him the $50 on an app, and I watched as Keisha sat scared in the front seat. The night sky was calling and growing darker by the minute.

I hated being out here and thought of calling the driver back. He said he would be on call if I needed him for another $50. I told him, "Give me 10 mins and I will let you know."

He looked out for me and said, "Just so I know you gonna be good, you want some more comfortable shoes?"

"You got shoes in your car?" I asked. These drivers be doing the most for five stars.

"I'm a working man. I got some of everything. Give me $25 and you can use them." I sent him some more money to borrow the shoes. I also got his number, and he killed his lights as he waited for my call.

I walked closer to see a clearer view, but made sure to stay out of sight. James got out from the backseat with a jacket on, and what I think was a gun in his pocket pointed at Keisha's passenger door. She was crying and he told her through clinch teeth, "Shut the fuck up. Get out the car."

She got out the car and the guy in the driver's seat got out, too. The three of them walked around to the back of the building. I couldn't see from here, but it didn't sound good. I don't know why I wore this dress out here, again; she had me looking like a duck during hunting season, and I hated it.

I tried to get closer to hear what I could or see something, I'm glad I wasn't wearing the wedges, I had no time to fall or step on a needle back here. I could see through the fence, and the wild bush behind me gave me some coverage. I had on a thin jacket that would give me a few minutes just to make sure she was good before I headed home.

This girl is so dang expensive. She and the guy are in the back with James, and he asks, "What the hell are you doing, Keisha?"

"Nothing. We aren't doing nothing," she replied

as James towered in her face.

"That's not what it looks like to me," says James.

The guy was silent and calm he said nothing. about James attitude or tone. If he is supposed to be the bigger fish, I sure enough can't tell. I thought it was odd, but I kept watching. "Keisha, do you know what you are doing to yourself? Do you know who the hell I am?"

"I was just having dinner, James. I didn't sleep with him or anything like that."

"Bitch you think I am worried about you sleeping with him. You ain't my woman, I don't give a dang what you do. My issue is you telling him my business."

Keisha looks worried but says, "What you mean?"

"I mean you opening up your mouth talking bout my shit," James barks.

"James, but I didn't say anything."

Then the man says, "That's not true. You were willing to tell me an earful if I gave you what you wanted."

"You little, bitch. You gonna say that. You know dang well I didn't have anything to say," replied Keisha.

James says, "I know you didn't know anything too important. But if you want to work for me, you first have to prove your loyalty. The little you thought you knew, you gave up on a cheap dinner, and I know some lame sex."

"But it's not like that," replies Keisha.

Her date says, "It's exactly like that. You would have sold your soul for some red bottoms, Keisha, come on."

"Really? After what I did to you?"

"You were aight. I had better," replies the man.

Keisha's spidey sense kicked in, and she realized she was cornered. I could see it on her face. Despair and then rage kicked in to give her the energy to run. She took off in the shoes she was wearing. I moved to get out of the bushes, and when I cleared the bushes, there was John.

"Hey, Rain, you really need to get home."

"I gotta go help, Keisha. I am not going home yet."

"Let me help you. You need to go home. If James knows you are here, you are bringing yourself in this. I don't know what this is, but I don't want you in it. Go home, please." He looks at me, and I can read his eyes. I didn't have much time to agree. I agreed.

I saw him quickly disappear from the bushes and follow the commotion behind Keisha. She was like a sheep being cornered by three wolves. Although one might have been a vegetarian, I don't know what it would mean to be in the pack with the others. I couldn't think about that, I just had to pray that he got to her before they did.

Relieved, I got to the car, and he said, "I figured you would need me." I gladly paid the $50 and headed home. I was on pins and needles, but I knew to call would only be a distraction. I had to deal with my own thoughts tonight. I couldn't look like an issue was ongoing as I entered the door, so I put on the best smile. I gave my mother my leftovers because I couldn't eat.

I told her I had a great time but was tired, and if we could speak in the morning. She happily agreed as she sat and ate the food I had gifted. I entered my room and quickly undressed. I put on my black pants and hoodie. Switched out my shoes, and I sat there waiting. Not sure of what I was waiting for but I knew the phone would ring.

I started to pray because my nerves were flying around like bats. "Lord, I don't know what is going on. I need you to step in, Father and help me, help Keisha, protect John. Father, may you bring your light into this dark place. May you be the greater in this situation. May you order my steps, God."

I kept hearing the prayer replay in my heart until I heard the phone. I went to it and it was a number I didn't recognize. I answered, "Hello?"

"Rain, it's Keisha. I need your help."

"Where are you? I am on 5th and Addison. Can you come and get me?"

"Yeah, I gotta call a ride. It might take a minute."

"Okay, I will look for you." I hung up and called the same driver. He wasn't far, so he came pretty quickly. I told my mom I forgot something at the restaurant and would be right back. She nodded, and I headed for the door. Quickly, I got into the car, and we sped off. I arrived in the area, but didn't see her. We drove down a bit farther, but still didn't see her. I asked him to "Park real quick, and I will walk around."

I got out and walked in a warmer outfit and maybe with a clearer head. I didn't see anything or hear anything at first. Then I heard it, I ran up the block, but stopped behind a building. Looking around the corner, I saw James, her date and John all three standing there.

John was speaking to James and he said, "James, come on. She is just a kid. You really think this was going to be something other than this anyhow?"

"I actually liked this little bitch, John. I wanted to believe she was going to be like a Brittany to me."

"But we don't have to do this. She is young and

dumb. I know you can see that. I am sure she learned a lesson, and we can just let her go."

"Let her go? John, you know dame well we can't do that. Dad taught us to tie up loose ends."

"But this doesn't have to be. We can send her away. We can do things differently. This is what Dad wanted, and you know it. For us to change some-things."

"That man wasn't our dad, John. This is our family. And women like her are a threat to that."

Keisha was bleeding and gagged sitting on the ground. She looked sweaty, and her eyes were the only thing that could speak for her. She had scraped up knees, and I wanted so badly to run over and grab her. To tell her it was going to be okay, but I knew I couldn't. I watched helplessly, praying things would work out. I knew this was beyond me.

"Come on, James. Can you do this for me? Can you let her go?"

"You want me to do this for you?"

"I mean–she's young."

"We were young. I could never get away with no shit like this, and I'm sorry bro, neither can she." Pop! I heard it but didn't see it. Her date shot her in the back. She slumped over sideways and started to bleed out there in the parking lot. I held my hands over my mouth to keep myself from screaming.

I couldn't unsee what I just saw. I prayed that she was somehow still alive. I knew when they left, I could put her in the car and drive her to the nearest hospital, and she could be alright. But next, James said, "You think you don't have to touch none of this shit, huhn? That you get to play with numbers, talk to police, and you don't have to worry about dirtying your hands."

James continues, "But let me tell you, you ain't no better than us. You are just like us. Tonight, you become one of us." James pulls the gun out of his pocket and points it at John. John looks surprised and says, "What the hell, James?"

"Like I said, you ain't no better than me, or Keith. We all in this life together. Pick her up." He looks at James longer, and James points the gun at Keisha and fires again. Her body jumps on the ground as the bullet ricochets within her flesh. John reads the warning shot, and he goes to pick up a wounded Keisha.

She was moving some, so all hope wasn't lost as he tried to pick her up. She could be saved! I watched on, and I wasn't sure why James wanted him to pick her up. Her blood rolls down his shirt, onto his shoes, and pants. He couldn't help but see her eyes; he started crying.

No moans, just silent tears. James sees the tears and says, "See this is the shit dad told you to stop.

She is the enemy, John. Snitches like her would be how you get killed. You cannot go soft. Dad went soft, and look at where that got him."

James continues, "You know that little bitch that killed our father, the one dad let go, he went back to camp and came after me. He didn't stop. He came back, and when he did, Dad stood in front of that bullet for me because he remembered the first rule. Never turn your back on your enemy."

"He regretted that shit, and I ain't gonna be like him. I ain't turning my back on my enemy, and neither will you. Throw her ass in the dumpster." John looks at him, and he puts his hand on the trigger again. John threw her in the dumpster, and Her body thuds as it hits the bottom. The dumpster seemed mostly empty or filled with light trash based on the noise.

He moves to walk away, and James says, "Not so quick, you're not done."

"What else am I supposed to do, James?"

He tosses him a lighter, "Light it and throw that bitch in there."

"Wait, you want me to do what?"

James, sensing his hesitation, takes a second shot at the dumpster, "Toss the dame lighter, John." John reluctantly lights the lighter and tosses it into the trash. Behind him is an instant roaring fire. I guess she wasn't drenched in sweat, but gasoline. It was like a bonfire was started in the dumpster, the flame flared so quickly, latching on to any cardboard or paper in the trash.

The crackling from the dumpster made my knees weak. I almost passed out where I stood, and I felt someone come up behind me and grab me. I wasn't sure of the fate of my heart or the circumstances. I closed my eyes and wished that the last 30 minutes hadn't happened, and I had gotten here sooner.

I didn't think of my safety immediately, but now that my eyes were dark and I could feel myself being carried, I thought to scream. But I recognized the shoes; it was my driver. He was here running me back to the car. He dropped my limp body in the backseat, and he gently took off with his lights off. I felt my body moving in the backseat as he took turns.

I lay on the seat, looking up at the ceiling, silently crying. I was muted this whole time, like I was still in shock. I couldn't process the tears or get out the cry. I felt an instant rush of images of Keisha, her being young, and then thinking of her mom, I couldn't hold it back anymore. I screamed, and I am not sure if I scared the driver.

I kept feeling the car move, and I knew I would get home, but I was afraid of what could wait for me when I got home. How could I go to work tomorrow? How could I look at John? What was I supposed to do? Who could I tell?

I was lost and I didn't know what to do. I couldn't do nothing, but nothing seemed like the only thing to do. I had to go into work and pretend everything was fine when I knew what I saw. James is a monster and John, John is powerless against him. I wasn't protected. I realized for the first time how vulnerable I really was.

I prayed harder for a way out. I didn't see it, but staying in was not an option. I needed God more than I have ever thought I would. I didn't want just the God who could give me gifts, get me into heaven, I wanted the one who could save me now. Save me from this mess, their messes. I needed God and that was the only name I could think to call on in that moment.

I was concerned for my mother. What would her tomorrow be like if I told her a word of what I saw tonight? She couldn't be different. I can't tell her anything. It was just between me, God, and the driver. I don't even know how much he saw. What if he said or did something?

Would I have to tell on him? Should I delete his phone number so there was nothing I could do to get back to him? But what if something happened to him? How could I help him after him saving me?

My mind was a sea of thoughts. I didn't know what to think or what to do. I let the car just drive and I grew more lost in my thoughts. My prayers became more powerful than my fears. My hope became more promising than the bleak outcomes I could play in my mind.

I had to believe everything I had learned over these years about God or I needed to trust something else. But on a day like today, I was assured of what I had hoped for. This is a divine encounter, a moment for God to be bigger than me and the outcomes. I couldn't do anything else but pray.

The car rolled to a slow stop, and I sat up. He opened the door and said, "Hey, you need to get out and quickly get up to your door." I nodded, but I was still dazed. He helped me up and I walked like he said, quickly. I'm guessing neither one of us knew if we were followed. I felt like he did circle the block a few times because it took longer for me to get home than to get there.

I kept my hoodie down and went around the back and not directly to my house. I wasn't sure who could have been watching me. I sat there for a few minutes until the lights went out, and then I walked up to my apartment and went inside. I didn't turn on the lights when I entered. I kept it dark. I went to my room and didn't take off my clothes.

I laid across my bed and I cried again. As hot tears ran down my face, I knew this marked a shift in my life. Have you ever gone through something that you knew would change you forever? This was the third day that my life would change again for-ever. Here I was trying to picture a life with dating included, and now, I am faced with the reality of that being a fantasy I had from the beginning.

I wanted to be yoked with someone who wasn't going in my direction, and the destructive path that could have been mine also I saw unfolded. A mistake could be what separated me from a dumpster set ablaze, too. Who could save me if James thought I was a threat? How much could I really be silent on?

What was I thinking? I had to pump the brakes on whatever I thought would be, and realize what I came to do. Make money to provide a better life for me and my mother. Making friends would have been a bonus, but this is way more than I bargained for.

I have to pray for direction for how to remove my grip on this family. My dreams of being a forever friend to John, and maybe something more, in that moment, vanished. He would remain forbidden fruit. A love never quenched.

YOU'RE ON THE ROLLER COASTER NOW

Going to sleep that night, I don't think I did. I probably had bloodshot eyes if only someone were to look. I didn't know how to do this day. I thought I did, but I didn't. I was lost, I was hurting, and I was alone.

John didn't call or text me yet, and I was glad he hadn't. I don't know what I should have said. So many things about last night I don't think I should have known, and for him to ask meant too much. I knew James was watching him, and he did too.

He finally called about twenty minutes before I was set to leave the house, "Rain, hey." His voice sounded raspy and ill. "I don't know what was in the food, but I feel like shit. I know we ate the same thing, so I wanted to check on you."

Not sure of the right cue, I took the easy bait. "Yeah, I have been on the toilet all night. My stomach is in knots. I hate to call in."

"No, no, it's okay. I know if you feel as badly as I do, you need to rest. So I can handle things today, just give me a call and let me know how you feel later on."

Slowly, I responded, "Yeah, of course I will. And thanks." We hung up the phone, and I knew this was a gift from God. If I had to go in, I don't think I could hold water. I don't think I could stop crying or keep my questions to myself. How can I look at John and not ask?

I knew how I felt, but I hadn't once thought about how he felt. He did plead for her life. He was also held at gunpoint by his brother. This whole situation is twisted. I knew I couldn't leave the house and had to look sick even to my mom if I wanted to pass this lie. I called my mom and told her that I was sick and asked what I should take.

Her being the mom she was, she offered to come home and take care of me. She has always been such an attentive mom. I told her, "No, it's okay. I will sort it out." She would see me soon enough, and I couldn't look sad, although I could be in pain. My mom could always tell the difference between the two.

I sat on the couch and saw the Bible; I opened it to see what God might want to tell me now. The pages landed on Mark chapter four verse thirty (Mark 4:30).

30 And he said, "With what can we compare the kingdom of God, or what parable shall we use for it?

31 It is like a grain of mustard seed, which,

when sown on the ground, is the smallest of all the seeds on earth,

32 yet when it is sown it grows up and becomes larger than all the garden plants and puts out large branches, so that the birds of the air can make nests in its shade."

33 With many such parables he spoke the word to them, as they were able to hear it.

34 He did not speak to them without a parable, but privately to his own disciples he explained everything.

I sat there and tried to glean what the Father wanted to tell me in this scripture. I prayed for an understanding, and the only thing I could think of was how I was a mustard seed. I was small, I didn't have much or look like much on the outside. I reflected on how this mustard seed survived last night and would undoubtedly survive whatever this was.

I knew that God would take my experience and make it make sense. I kept reading to the end of the chapter, and it talked about Yashua, or Jesus, speaking to the wind. He asked, "How come his disciples still lack the faith to speak to the wind?" I didn't want faith to be the reason I could not win.

As the disciples were running around scared of the water in the boat, Yashua lay there fast asleep in peace because I am guessing he trusted God on this situation too. He learned to trust God, and the disciples were still worried about their circumstances. My situation, like the disciples on the boat, is very real.

But unlike the disciples, I wasn't going to run; I wasn't going to be afraid. I am choosing to trust God to show me the way out of this. I remember hearing in a sermon at church that God will make a way for our escape. I need an escape today, and so does John.

I didn't think about this, but I guess Keisha needed one, and her mother did too. But who would think that death is an escape? I can't imagine what her mom will feel, but I also can't imagine the stress she has had with a daughter who refused to listen or respect her. I don't think any mother would wish their children dead so they didn't have to deal with their nonsense. Most would gladly suffer for them.

It was a long day for me of thinking, praying, and reading. I don't think I ever did a more in-depth bible study to date. I was in it, reading the bible like it was a movie playing on tv. I was hooked, but was it fear that gripped me or sincere love of the words in the book? I wasn't sure, but I didn't care to find out either.

I turned on the tv and before I could get any-where, I turned it off. I couldn't risk seeing some-thing I couldn't unsee on tv. I never watched basic television, only network apps. But today, I knew I had to do something different. I turned to social me-dia to see what was happening. Not to my surprise, Keisha's mom was posting about her daughter.

She was asking had anyone seen her and if they had to contact her. I wondered if I was wrong to keep silent. I knew to say a word would put me and John at risk. I also knew what being silent could mean. I wasn't ready to make that decision, so I turned off the phone.

I looked out the window, and I heard a "knock" at the door. I knew who it was. I went to the door. I opened it, and John said, "You look like hell." Without a smirk, I said, "I feel terrible."

He asked to come in, and I moved to allow him entry. He sat on the couch, and he seemed really nervous. He just kept rubbing his pants legs. I knew he wanted to say something, but I didn't ask a question that I didn't already know the answer to. But not to ask would also make for more questions.

Unsure of what to say, I blurted out, "Did you find Keisha? Did she go back with James last night?"

"Yeah, ugh…" He grew more nervous and I knew he was shuffling his words in his mind. He was usually a cool-headed person, so this was new.

"I um, I tried to find her last night, but…but I think I am going to need some more time."

"Yeah? To find her?" I asked, trying to hold my tears back, although my voice cracked.

"Rain, I don't want you to worry. But I can't say that she will be okay when I find her."

"You think James did something to her?"

"I can't say that, but I just want you to trust me. I will do everything I can to protect you. You believe that, right?"

"Of course I do," I replied, still keeping my distance.

"I need you to follow my lead. When I tell you to leave or come, I need you to do that, alright?" I nodded in agreement. I knew what he was trying to do, although I questioned if he could do it, keep me safe.

"Well, I can't stay long. I gotta go, but I wanted to check on you." He gets up and starts to head for the door. I didn't sit because I couldn't. I was near the door, and he came to me and gave me a hug. His warm embrace was welcomed. I needed a hug. We hugged for what felt like a long while, then he walked out the door. I wasn't sure if that was his "I'm sorry hug" or not.

I grieved for him and prayed for him starting from that moment more. I didn't know what his day was like, but I figured it would be rough. He didn't say where he was going, but an hour later, I heard another knock on the door. I thought it was John coming back for something, but it wasn't.

I opened the door, and it was my neighbor, Keisha's mom. "Hey Rain, sorry to bother you. I know it is early. I just wanted to ask, have you heard from Keisha?"

"Today?"

"Well, she didn't come home last night. So I was just wondering if anyone had heard from her today?"

"No, I didn't today. I saw her yesterday. She was on a date, I think. We didn't speak long."

"Was she good?"

"Yeah, she told me to mind my own business and stop trying to be her bigger sister."

"I always appreciated that about you, Rain. You always looked out for her. If you hear from her, can you let her know to please come home?"

Without hesitation, I replied, "Of course." She thanked me and went down the stairs in search of the daughter, who I knew was already dead. I thought I was fine, but I wasn't. I went into muffled tears as I went to lie on my bed, and then I ran to the bathroom to threw up. I started to feel sick to my stomach.

I wondered how long before people would start asking more questions. She called me on a strange number, so would that call link back to me? Could I be somehow implicated in the murder of Keisha? I was spiraling again, worried as if I had done something wrong. I knew something, wasn't that a crime to say nothing?

But what would I say? How could I have the conversation? None of it was making sense. I had to chill out and right now focus on feeling better. I really did feel sick now.

A few hours later, my mom came home and she came straight to me to check on me. She asked, "Are you feeling better? Do you think you need to go to the hospital, Rain?"

"No, Mom. I am feeling much better." That was a bag of mixed truth. I was better because I saw her and knew she was good. I was not feeling better at all, but I was never really sick.

"You don't look too good."

I replied, "I know. It's been a long day, is all."

My mom then asked, "Hey, did you hear about Keisha?"

I tried to look puzzled, and my mom went on to say, "Yeah, her mom is looking for her. Searching the neighborhood and stuff. I think she will file a missing persons report tomorrow if she doesn't come home soon. But don't they make you wait seventy-two hours before you can file a missing person?"

"Mom, I don't know." I was gonna say more, but the vomit started to roll up my throat, choking out the lie I thought to tell. I ran to the bathroom and released the pressure. My mom came to the door, "Rain, you want me to make you something?"

No matter what she made, I am sure it wouldn't help what I had going on. I replied, "No, I think it is just passing. I should be alright just need some cold water."

"Okay, I will put a glass on the table for you. I saw John, he looks pretty bad too."

"Yeah?" I replied from the bathroom as I washed my face and picked up my toothbrush.

"Yeah, he asked about you. He seemed really concerned about you." She was moving things around in the kitchen and then said, "I told him I hadn't talked to you before I left for work, but knew you made it in because I saw you asleep on your bed."

I was brushing my teeth but managed to stop for a second and ask, "What else did you say?" Shoot, I pray she didn't tell him anything about me going out again last night. He must know? Naw, I am sure she didn't mention it I thought to myself as I finished brushing.

"I told him the next time he brings you back in so late, he needs to call to let me know. I would have missed work if he hadn't answered to let me know you were good."

I quickly spit out the water and almost hit the mirror. I wiped the mess I made and hollered back, "Oh, so you called when I left out?" I could feel my eyes bulging out from their sockets. I could have been inverted in that moment with how my emotions were running on this roller coaster I could not get off of. Being in the bathroom was the right place because I couldn't hide my reaction.

"Yeah, you said you would be right back, and you took a while. So I called him to check on you. I don't know why I didn't think to call you first."

That comment cemented what I had feared; he knew I had gone back for Keisha. The question I had was, did James know I went back? Did John try to save Keisha because he knew I was watching? Or did he get the call after I had already left? Did he know I saw Keisha's murder?

I was in a swarm of thoughts, and the vomit came rolling back up in my throat. I released it again in the toilet. I couldn't shake the feeling I was about to get a whopping, and I hated it. The vomit violently shook my body and I felt a little trimmer when it ended. I wanted to do what was right, but I wasn't sure of how to do that. I was getting scared, but I couldn't show my fear. There was no room for fear.

Regardless of whether I liked it or not, I was on this roller coaster, and I had to see it to the end. There was another knock on the door. I am tweaking now in the bathroom. How many knocks can there be in one day? It was Keisha's mom.

She was a single lady who never dated after Keisha's dad died, so with Keisha gone, I should have figured she would come here to speak to my mom.

The two of them were really good friends. She came in and she started talking about all the places she had looked. How she had called all her friends and tried to find her phone. The phone was off, but they did trace her phone to 8th Street.

She was saying her fears, "I am really scared something bad could have happened, Connie." My mom took her hands in hers and said, "Let's not think like that. Keisha is gonna be alright. Let's stay positive and believe that God will bring her back home."

Depending on where home is, she is already there. It was the hardest moment to hear people around me looking for the girl I knew had met her end. I didn't like being the person in on the secret. I would have gladly switched places with any of them to not know. But I wasn't them. She said she would keep on looking for her in the area.

A mother's intuition is something serious. She was near her final resting place and would soon find her, I knew it. What would this mean for John? James? Or me? And what about the driver?

I wanted to call him to see what he remembered. I thought maybe I didn't see what I thought, and this was a dream, a nightmare. I tried calling the number. He didn't answer. I thought again and wondered if it was right to keep calling him from my phone. As I debated how to be better at secrets, I heard the phone ring back.

"Hey, you alright?" It was the driver. I replied, "Yes, but I don't really understand what is going on."

"Don't worry. I called the cops and they know everything I saw. Those guys who harmed your sisters, they will find them."

Did he just say what I think he said? This is bad, real bad. I didn't want to root for the enemy here, but the enemy and the victim are both my friends. What do I do? How do I choose, or what story do I tell? How much of the story? Will I get in trouble, too, for not telling first?

The queasy feeling rose in my belly as I awaited the news. I wanted to call John so badly, to warn him, maybe? But that would be admitting I was there. I think he knows I was, could he be cleaning my tracks? Did he see me?

Why am I going crazy right now? "Rain," I gently hit myself on my thighs and said, "Get it together." I knew I needed to think, but so much was happening and I couldn't. I didn't know how to stop or slow the coaster down, although I wanted to.

I waited for the next call, and I could guess it would be John. If he didn't call me, I thought to go to him. I had to warn him about the beehive that was struck and the swarm of problems above his head. I would want someone to tell me if I punched a beehive. I just prayed he wasn't allergic to bees.

After not hearing from him, I called him. He

didn't answer, and I grew concerned. I guessed that when he played sick earlier, James was watching him. He must be with James. What does he have him doing now?

I guess it was safer for him to be with James because he could keep a watchful eye on him that way. I nervously waited for him to call me back. I got the call I was waiting for at about 9pm. "Hey, you alright?" It was John speaking in a rushed tone.

I replied, "Yeah. Just waiting to hear back from you." Then I asked, "Are you good?"

"Not really, I mean I am now."

"Did something happen?"

"I just got into a small fight. I will tell you about it when I see you. You busy now?"

"Just at the house with my mom."

"I think you need to come with me, just for tonight. You think your mom would allow that?"

"You want me to stay the night?"

"What did I tell you?"

"Alright. I will talk to her."

"I will be there in an hour." I went to my mom and told her the first thing that came to mind. I couldn't tell her the truth, because I didn't know what that was. I did the best I could do; I told her what I would do. "Hey, Mom."

She looks up from reading. She reads when she is tired of movies or doing her devotional. "Hmm?" She says without looking up. "I need to go by Mrs. Brittany's."

She finishes reading whatever she was reading, and looks to me. "Is everything alright?"

"Yeah, John is having to go out and asked for me to keep an eye on her overnight."

"You comfortable with that?"

"I mean, yeah. Mrs. Brittany is sweet. I am sure he just wants me to make sure she doesn't end up outside. I can handle that."

"Alright, but if it gets weird or to be too much, you call me."

"I will, Mom."

I was cleared by my mom, but I wondered about her, too. I asked for Keisha's mom to come over and keep her company for me. I needed another pair of eyes in case something happened, and I think she will need a friend if she got the news about her daughter. No one should hear that their child was found in a dumpster dead, alone.

I left out of the house when I saw the lights flash on John's car. I got in and instantly saw his bandaged hand. I wanted to ask what happened, but I sensed he might not be ready to talk about it yet. He looked forward and drove with intention. We got to the house, and he was looking around, I take it scanning the environment. For a guy who was green on things, he shifted gears real quick. We entered the house and he checked all the doors, windows, and on his mother, who was asleep.

He sat with me on the couch and didn't say a word. We just sat there and I didn't speak, but waited to hear him out. He leaned his head on my shoulder, and I held his head and patted him. He took several deep breaths as he just sat there. After a few moments, I said, "Are you alright, John?"

"No, this shit is just getting worst—sorry Rain. I know you don't cuss. I just feel tired."

"It's cool. I get it. What happened to your hand?"

"I got into a fight with James."

"Really? About what?"

He waits a few moments and says, "You."

"Me?" Oh, no. They know I was there. My anxiety started rising again. I had to take a deep breath and focus on listening. He went on to say, "I know you were there."

My heart sank. The roller coaster just fell on a drop, and I had nowhere to run. I tried to play stupid because any other turn didn't leave nowhere to run. "Where?" I didn't deny it, but also didn't confirm it.

"I know you were there, Rain. I feel like shit because I couldn't stop it. I was too scared and I hate myself for it. For what I did."

"But you didn't do anything." I started crying as I felt his warm tears roll down his face. I knew I could let my guard down, too.

"I really tried to save her, I really did, Rain. I don't want you to see me like this. I am not a monster, Rain. This is why I told you to stay away from him. Too many people who get close to him die. I never wanted that for you." As he poured out his heart, I rocked him like a baby.

"I know. This isn't your fault."

"But it is my fault. I should have done more to keep Keisha away. I shouldn't have left that day. I should have fought that day, then maybe we wouldn't be here."

"Another man's mistakes are not yours, John."

"That is not how it has been for me. James' mistakes are mine. My dad's mistakes have been mine. I am paying for too many men's mistakes, and I am not gay. This isn't stuff I chose, or ever wanted for myself. I hate how people keep taking advantage of me and expect me to take it."

He was silent for a little longer and then he said, "I am tired. I'm tired of being the weak one, the one who runs. The one everyone wants to take a shit on."

"I don't think you are weak. And I know you are not gay. Sometimes we have to take a hit for the team or we can feel like going through is punishment. But we can choose to change things, John."

"Nobody has no idea of what I wanted to tell my dad that day. No one would listen. There is so much shit I could say--and need to say."

"I'm here. Whatever you want to talk about, I am here to listen." He grew quiet for a few moments. I heard his breathing slow, and his body became more relaxed. He sat up and he wiped his face. He looked at me and said, "I have been wanting to tell someone this for years. But no one would stop long enough to hear me. They all thought they knew what had happened, but never asked me."

He went on, "My brother didn't ask me. My dad didn't wait long enough for me to tell him. My mother was more concerned about other stuff, and had no time. I wanted so badly to tell my dad, but he shut me down." The room grew silent.

THE DARK ROAD IS LONELY

John draws in a deep breath with a curled back and he says, "I used to lie awake in my bed many nights for years, wondering what the night would bring. I used to hear noises in the house. People screaming and wild things I cannot explain. I didn't know what was going on but I also knew I couldn't tell just anyone either. I knew my parents had a dark secret, but I tried to pretend I didn't see it."

I listened intensely as he began to bare his soul.

John's Flashback...

There was a thump on the floor. I heard it and a crash of yelling. I heard my mom screaming and my dad saying, "Stay out of this." I don't know the details of the conversation, but I used to find comfort in going to my neighbor's house. His house was quiet, and I could crawl on his AC and easily get in through the window.

He was a boy a few years older than me. I might have been around 6, and he was 8 or 9. His parents were very different from mine. They hardly ever fought, and it wasn't a commotion I ever heard sleeping on the floor in his room. We would be up talking about dinosaurs and crap we've seen on tv. Nothing crazy, but all in boy fun.

We did this for years. When I was ten, I was big enough not to need the AC unit. I could get in through the window with him pulling me up. One day, he pulled me up, and I landed on top of him when we fell. It was awkward, and I apologize for the landing. He told me not to apologize, and it was cool.

I didn't think no more about it. We hung out and talked like usual, but I had fallen asleep. This boy was bigger than me, he was more cooler than me, but he kept to himself like I did after school. We were best friends, although he didn't hang out with me too much at school. I liked hearing his stories because I knew the chances of me becoming popular were not likely.

His life was my great escape and the person I wanted to become. I wanted a regular family. One where I could be myself. Go to school and be cool. Be attractive. On that night, I fell asleep quickly, and I felt him try to lie beside me. I got up out of my sleep quickly and stood up.

"Dude, what are you doing?" I said in a quiet whisper.

"Don't tell me you don't like me, too?" He replied.

"What the hell? Man, I ain't gay."

"You have been jumping in my window almost every night. Why else would you do that?"

"Because my parents argue or have company over. I don't want to hear that shit. When they ain't yelling, they are having you, know, sex. Trust me, you don't want to hear that either. But I am not gay."

"So you don't like me?"

"Not like that. We are best friends, but no, I am not gay."

"What if you are gay?"

"I'm not."

"But how would you know?"

"Know I am not gay?"

"No, I mean, know if you are. Have you ever thought about it?"

"No, man. I ain't gay. There is nothing to think about. My dad would kill me."

"So, is that why you haven't thought about it? Because of your dad?"

"No, because I don't think about being with a boy."

"Do you think about being with a girl?"

"I don't think about being with nobody. I am ten!"

"I'm thirteen. So what? We know when we know. I like you."

I started to back up from him. And he tired to get closer, but I went for the window. I jumped out so quick. I hoped I didn't break anything, but I got up with an awkward limp that carried into the next day. I walked it off, but I wasn't going to his room again after that.

My brother saw me coming out the window that night, he must have. I am not sure if he told my dad, but he did see me. He started to make gay jokes and call me fagot and stuff. He must have thought we had sex because I was limping the next day. We got into a big fight a few days later, and when my dad asked what was going on, we both said nothing.

Things went on like this for months. I hated the life my best friend gave me. It was a complete mis-understanding that I wanted to clear the air with my dad. When he asked me to talk to him, I wanted to tell him what happened. I wanted to have an honest conversation. I wanted to know if I was gay because of my actions or was I the gay type because I wasn't like James.

The conversation wasn't about the boy; it was about me. When he shut me down, that sucked the life out of me. I started to think more about the conversation my neighbor and I had. I wanted my dad to rescue me to reassure me of my confessions and beliefs, but I didn't get that. I wanted James, to see me and pick up for me. But he just saw me as his little gay brother.

I heard him tell people that at school, too. The school started saying that I was his "gay brother," and I was in a box. The girls thought I was gay and wouldn't talk to me. My neighbor tried to apologize but I was pissed. I didn't talk to him for like two years. Then one day, something happened at my house that was very bad news. I had to get out of the house. But I had nowhere to go.

I knew there were deals happening in the house and other bad things. That night I heard a gunshot, I was sure of it, and I needed to tell someone. I couldn't keep a lid on it anymore. Reluctantly, I went to my neighbor's house and I spilled the beans. Not on everything, but enough. I just talked about the screams and the things that made me scared. I was thirteen and I didn't know what to do.

The boy wasn't my friend at all. He heard all of my story and devised a plan. I was coming home one day after school, and he saw me. "Hey, come by tonight, I have something to tell you." I didn't think much of it. Night came, and I went by his window. I stood outside his window and I said, "Hey, what's up?"

He said, "I was thinking about what you said. I think you should tell the cops."

I almost jumped out of my skin, "Call the cops? Are you crazy?"

"No, if you are in deep shit like this, you need to get out of there."

"Man, I am not calling the cops. These are my parents. This is my life, not no fairytale. Where would I go exactly?"

"You can choose where you go."

"That's some white shit. We can't do that. Snitches get stitches, and black parents, you don't call on them unless your life circumstances is unbearable. What I am going through is normal."

"No, it ain't. You can come live with me. Stay with us."

"No disrespect, but I would never fit in there."

"Why don't you try it. You can have a regular life like we talked about."

"That's not what I meant. I want to have a regular life with my family, not yours or anyone else's. I don't need a new family, I want to be loved by my family. Don't you get it?"

He genuinely looked confused but he said, "I can be your family. We can be together." And that's when he almost kissed me, and I turned my face. "What the hell? I thought we talked about this already. I am not gay!"

"Then why do you keep coming around? Why does everyone say you gay? Are you gay and just don't like me? What? Because I am white?"

"No, because I am not gay man. Look, forget you ever knew me."

"Is that what you want? For me to forget that your parents might be a crime family? How do you think the cops would feel about that? You think they would want to know that, John?"

"Don't do this, bro. I am telling you. That would be the worst mistake you make."

"Like you said, forget you ever knew me, too. Next time you hear a noise, stay in your own dame room since you got it all figured out." He turned and left back through his window. I looked up and saw my brother standing there. I am guessing he was sneaking in late from a date he had.

I didn't say a word, I just turned and went into the house. He knew that I had talked to the guy next door and heard the threat. I couldn't stop the ball from rolling. I knew soon he would tell my dad what he saw and heard. But what he told my dad was not what happened.

After that, he pulled your mom from me. I had no best friends, and my brother was convinced I was gay. I was alone. I had no one. My mother loved me, but she was busy doing whatever my dad wanted, and it felt like it was everyone against me.

My brother didn't let what the neighbor said slide either. He and his crew jumped the boy real bad a few days later and scared his parents so badly that they moved. If I wanted to apologize, I couldn't. The chance was taken, and I wondered if I should have been gay. Was that why I suffered so much? Was this God's way of punishing me for even thinking about it?

Back to…

"I just didn't want to be alone. Was there really something wrong with that? He cried more in my arms as I rocked him. I knew this was long overdue, and I didn't want to stop his process. But I knew I had to tell him what I saw and had learned about the night.

"Tonight, Rain, I know that besides my mother, you are the only person I have ever cared about more than myself. I know we are not dating or something serious, but I would give my life for yours." I saw it in his eyes; he was serious.

"John, why are you talking like this?"

"Because you make me feel seen, no matter what happens. I want you to know I mean this. I know everyone thinks I am this wimpy guy because I don't shoot people or sleep with a lot of women. I am not a virgin, but I am selective. I just want it to mean something. You know?"

I nodded and said, "I can understand that. I haven't done it yet."

"Good. I thought it was just me," he replied.

I started to kid, "Wait, you just said you had?"

"I couldn't be the one to admit it first. Of course, I am a virgin. It just never happened." We shared another moment of light fun, and I almost forgot the news I needed to share.

"But John, I gotta tell you something." The laughter broke off and he knew the situation was turning too.

"Uhuhn, yeah?"

"I did see you last night," I continued to say.

"So, you were there the whole time?"

"Yeah. I was there. I called a ride, but I didn't go home. I had him follow Keisha's car."

"I told you, Rain, to go home."

"I know, and I tried, but I waited around to be sure she was good. I saw what the guy did and your brother."

Slowly, he said with eyes downcast, "And what I

did too, right?"

Quietly, I replied, "Yeah. I saw what you did, too."

"Shit, Rain. I–"

"I need you to know that the driver saw it too."

"The driver?"

"Yeah, when things were happening, he got me from the bushes and took me home. He told me today that he reported it."

"Shit, shit. Rain, do you know what this means?"

"I don't know, John?" I got scared watching his movements. He popped up and started shifting around. He looked like he wanted to scream, but he kept holding it back. I didn't know how to be there for him in this moment. So I could only watch on.

"Okay, so do you feel like he would be able to ID all of us?"

"I don't know. Not likely, right?"

"But if he doesn't ID me and us, then they might call you as a witness. If they call you as a witness, what would you do?"

"What are you saying, John? Why would they

call me?"

"Rain, don't you get it. You were at a crime scene that puts me, my brother, and Keith at the scene. You know our names, faces, and everything. They are likely going to come and talk to you."

I replied nervously, "But John, I don't know what to say."

He paces the floor and nods his head. The plan was formulating in his mind and with confidence he says, "Don't worry about it. I got it, you won't have to say nothing."

"But you just said I would be questioned?"

"Not if I could make it all go away."

"What are you going to do? Kill the driver?"

"No, Rain, no. This is a done deal. I will have to turn myself in."

"Why would you do that? This is James's fault and even Keith's. Not yours."

"That won't matter. If they pin James or Keith, it will only open up more worms. If James skips town, I don't know about you being safe if I am free. He will assume I snitched, and you are as good as dead."

I heard the word "dead."

"Dame, I wanted him to be wrong," he said.

"Wrong about what?"

"About you." He said as he breathed out slowly. I looked at him, looking for an explanation. He continued, "He told me today caring about you would get me killed or in jail."

"So what does that mean?"

"I made it mean nothing. I told you I would do anything for you. And whatever he thought to do to you, I would never allow!"

"What the hell, John! He wants to kill me?"

"Calm down. He just sees you as a loose end. But I told him you were good."

"Oh, and you are going to save me like you did Keisha?"

"Come on, that's not fair, and you know it. That girl had this coming to her without my help. She would have slept her way up to a crime boss if she could smell the trail to find one, and you know that. I fought James for you, because I told you, I wouldn't let nothing happen to you. He didn't make it out that room did he?"

I knew what he was saying was true but it didn't change the facts. "So what did you do, John?"

214

"We got into a fight. He swung, then I swung. He tried to shoot, but I shot first."

"Wait, so you killed your brother John?"

"No, I grazed him. He is probably at some clinic getting stitched, same as I was. We both fine."

"And what do you think is going to happen when he gets out?"

"He might come by here."

"And you bring me here?"

"You think it would be better for us to be at your house?"

He was right, I wouldn't want to bring this drama to my momma's house. We sat there trying to figure it out. He said, "If I confess to the murder, there would be no need for an investigation. This would be a closed book. James will skip town, and he won't look back. He will think I ratted on him, and he won't come back neither will Keith."

"So you think the solution is to let the murderers go? Please tell me I'm missing something. No, tell on the bad guys and let them go to prison."

"This life doesn't work like that. We all carry debt. When someone dies or turns up missing, whatever they were doing doesn't stop. Whoever is on top would be next to pop or come and collect from. If we are both in the wind, there is no one left; there is nothing else to do but move on."

"I don't understand this."

Cool as a new autumn breeze, he replied, "I am gonna clear up the liabilities, and when it's done. I am going to need a favor."

"Don't you think this is all crazy, John? Just think for a second. You see what kind of man your brother is, and why would you save him?"

"Someone's got to... My dad told me to."

"Your dad told you to go to prison for him?"

"No, he was telling me I was stronger than my brother and to cover him. He was different in those last few years. He told me he got me."

John's Flashback...

It was that time when my brother had gone out the door after that fight between him and our dad. My dad called to me while I was in the kitchen, and I came in and sat down in the living room on the couch. He was in his favorite spot, and he said, "I get you, John." Confused on what he was talking about, I replied, "What, Dad?"

"I get what you have felt all these years. I see what it was like for you with James, heck with me too." I didn't comment because I wasn't sure where the direction was going. He continued to talk, so I took a seat. "I used to think like James. I heard myself, and I left no room for anyone to think differently. I was so convinced that my way was the only way that I blocked out anyone who did something differently."

He hit it on the head, now what I thought. He said, "I know you don't trust me. I know you are still as skeptical of me as James. But I am a different man, John. I am not who I used to be, and that is only thanks to Yah. I don't want my family to miss seeing the man God has made me to become. Can you help me?"

"Help you do what, Dad?" I honestly didn't know what I could do to help him. My mom was on her journey of isolation. My dad was closed off from James, his number one son, and he was left with me. The son everyone swore was the screw up and the gay faggot of the family. He said, "I am sorry I didn't hear you out. If you are gay, or thought you were, I should have heard you. If you wanted to talk about anything, I should have stopped to listen. Now, here I am trying to talk about something that is different, and no one will hear me."

I sat there and stared at him for a minute, "I hear you, Dad," I said. He nodded and said, "Thank you. I really did my best to make sure you didn't ruin your life. I thought this was the life. We had things, money, power, and lived in a big house. This is what the dream was all about. I wanted to protect it for you, but not use it as a prison. I know I failed at that."

I listened and didn't say anything. He said, "I know now, that you standing up to me and being willing to be open about something that was personal wasn't easy. I get it now. That you telling me something I didn't want to hear, had to be hard for you. I don't know if you are gay or not, and it is not a big issue for me anymore. I let my fear run you off as my son. I should have been there for you, but I ran."

He was right again. What is talking through my dad, because this is nothing like him I remember thinking. He was kind, understanding, and thoughtful. I wanted him to keep talking, but he got a phone call that I knew would end the conversation. I was so close to having closure, I thought about this long standing lie.

Could having the conversation we needed to years ago, fix what we felt was the disconnect now? I didn't have that answer then, and I still wonder about that question now. But what he said before leaving the room was, "John, remember, family stays there. No matter what people say, who lied, or who leaves our side. True family keeps hope alive and does what they can to protect the family. I get that now. And I promise, I will do everything I can to make things right with you."

Then like that, he was gone.

Back to today...

I cannot say I understood all the moments in the story, but I saw what it meant to John. He had been living under a lie all these years. James knew, or maybe he didn't clearly see, and thought he did. Maybe he needed something on John, because he was jealous? John was smart, an artist, his mother loved him, and he was a good kid.

Siblings do stupid stuff to level the playing field within the family; maybe this was that for him. To show him as flawed in this cruel way? I don't really know, I am no doctor, but it smells like a sibling rivalry gone wrong for too long.

I tried to suggest other ways to think about this, but he denied them all. He told me to go upstairs with his mother and stay there until he calls me. I did what he said. I went to his mother's room, and she was fast asleep. I prayed not to wake her as I tiptoed into the room. I lay on her empty couch with my eyes wide open; I couldn't sleep.

I wasn't sure what John was going to do, and if he would do what he said, or if I needed to believe it. I didn't know what to say, or who to blame. I was stuck in a horrible place, and only God could dig me out. Dig out John and sort out James and the others. I dreaded the morning because I knew Keisha's death would be announced, and that could not be undone.

What the driver had done would prove she was murdered, and a case would ensue until they closed it. I must have fallen asleep at some point in the night. My body was tired even though my mind was racing. I woke up hearing the bathroom faucet. I gently woke up and allowed myself to slow down and be in the moment.

Brittany came out of the bathroom and said, "Good morning? You must have come up early. You have been sleeping for hours."

"Oh, sorry, Ms. Brittany." I was embarrassed because I was there to help her, and here she is helping me.

"No, it's alright. I had a few drunken nights during my day, too. No judgment here. I am hungry, though." I giggled a little and said, "Yes, of course. Let me go get your breakfast."

I didn't know the time or what was going on. I went to the bathroom and freshened up. John had left me a toothbrush and things I needed. I went to the kitchen and on the counter I saw a carton of muffins and a note. I put the note in my pocket and enjoyed a muffin. One time, we went to breakfast, and he thought of giving me this extravagant meal. I said, "A muffin would have been cool too."

I don't know how he knows what to do at the right times, but he does. I enjoyed that muffin as much as I could have. It was the right bite for what I needed to keep moving. I feared eating anything more, might turn into a ball of discomfort in moments to come.

It was an eerie morning. I checked the time because last night felt like a black out. It was 10:30am. Normally, I am up around 7am, so I must have been tired. I saw that my mom had called. She sent me a text to call her when I had a minute. I figured the news, so I pushed off the call.

Likely, she wasn't coming in and was staying back to be with Keisha's mom. It was me and Ms. Brittany today, and whose to say if this would become more of the norm? I wondered if John would be in or if he was still in the house. I made breakfast and served Ms. Brittany first.

She was thankful and watched her tv as she ate. I went down and grabbed a plate for John, hoping yesterday was sleep deprivation speaking. I knocked on his door and didn't hear him. I figured he was gone, but I wanted to check.

I went back downstairs and sat at the table. The plate I made for him became a picture I took. I thought to share it on social because I knew I couldn't eat it. I turned on my phone and I went on y social page. Before I could scroll, I saw it. The article was everywhere.

"Girl Found Dead in Dumpster," "Breaking News: Girl Found Dead In Dumpster," "Ongoing Investigation..." I stopped reading, looking. This was the nightmare I feared, and I woke up in it.

I wondered if his mother knew anything about it; likely not. I am sure he doesn't talk this kind of business with her anymore. I sat there, dumbfounded and uncertain of my next move. The only move certain was to call my mother.

As predicted, she was with her best friend. They were called to verify the body, and my mom has been with her since the morning when she got the call. She was strong on the phone, but I knew this was a shock to her, too. She was the woman assuring her friend that her daughter was safe, now she is the same woman who is with her to verify her daughter's dead body. It was a sharp turn of events, and I feared what my role in it could bring more fallout.

Before I could get lost on my rabbit trail of thoughts, I got a call from an unknown number. I was wary of answering it, considering the news articles, but I answered nervously, "Hello?"

"Hey Rain," it was John. "I know you see the articles. I wanted to tell you, don't worry. I am not there because I didn't want them to come there looking for me and tear up the house. It would break my mother's heart. I left you a note on the table, that's in your pocket, read it. It will give you everything you need."

I looked at the time; it was before noon. I wondered, "Did he get any sleep?" How could he be so put together? In a calm voice, he said, "I gotta go. But I will call you again soon. Please tell my mom I love her, and I will try to see her. She is not good with goodbyes. So don't make it sound so final."

"Wait, John. Where are you?"

"Where I told you I would be. The last place James would come."

"You at the station?"

"I love you, Rain. Bye, and read the note. Call you later," then John hung up. What was the ending of this? When the phone hung up, it felt so final. The air was clearing, and fear was subsiding. I knew it would be moments before John would hit the papers. I felt terrible for him.

It just seemed like his life was a roller coaster of bad news after the next. I didn't know how God could change his life, change his circumstance, but I prayed that he would. I sat there and I opened the letter, and started to read it.

"Rain, I pray you know that you have been a whirlwind in my life. You have come into this house and, with your quirky ways, made a space in my heart. If I could ever show you my gratitude or my love, I wouldn't hesitate to do both."

I paused reading as I cleared my throat, "I left you with power of attorney for my Mom, if you will accept it. I know my brother is gone. I told him everything, and he left for good this morning. I settled accounts, so no one will be here for anything. If they come, they are liars. Send them to my lawyers at the bottom of the note, and he will deal with it."

"If something should happen to me, you are my beneficiary. And my only request is that you please take care of my mother, and if you can, look after James from a distance. I love you, Rain. Thank you for being the best part of my life. I don't know if you know, but I listen to you, and I am doing this for you. Love, John."

I couldn't hold it anymore, it is real. He is gone. How could he admit he killed a woman he didn't kill? Why would he lay his life down like this? Why God? Why would you take him from us? I cried at that kitchen table all afternoon. I stayed with his mother, and all I could do was tell her she would see him again, but I had no idea of when or how soon.

Later that evening, I got a call from the jail. "Hey, I am booked and this is my phone call, can you put my mom on?" I darted to give her the phone. She answered, and her smile lit up at hearing his voice.

You could see how much the two of them mean to each other, and I could understand, looking at her, how much pain Keisha's mom was in. To think she could never call her daughter, no matter her life decisions, had to be hard, too. My mom was between a rock and a hard place, knowing John and seeing her best friend.

She knew how to walk the line and be there for them both. I went to see him, and she came with me. It was nice to see him, but also difficult. He didn't look well. I knew he had been sick before growing up, but I never saw him look so withdrawn. It was like his eyes were sinking in, and his skin was tight.

He looked different and seemed way more somber. I wondered if he had regretted his choice, but he assured me he hadn't. My mom wanted to ask why he did it, but she knew as soon as she saw him, he didn't. She had no questions, only prayers for him.

He thanked her, but he told her, "Not much prayer can do for me in here." He kidded but it was like a knife in my heart. I wanted him to have hope because hope was all he could have in here. He needed a shoulder to lean on and I couldn't be that for him in here.

I wrote him each day. He didn't want his mom to come there to see him, but he made some recordings for her and left them with me. The thumb drive was full of voice memos made while I sat there. I saw with each visit him fading. It burned my heart, and I wanted to bring up God, and when I tried, he would just assure me that there was no need.

I think he felt he deserved what he was getting. "John, the truth is we all deserve what we have to deal with. We all deserve to live a life of hell, but who could survive? Who could endure a burden like that?"

"Rain, my dad talked about that, and that didn't save him either. In the end, he died."

"But what did your father say? Family sticks around when others leave. John, we are family. I will be around, no matter what. You are not alone anymore." He placed his hand on the window and walked away. Some visits were easier than others.

I felt bad that at sometimes I didn't want to go. Not because I didn't want to see him, I wasn't sure of what to say. I didn't know how to ease his pain. I didn't know how to show my gratitude. I wrote him letters, but none of them filled the hole in my heart. I thought his brother would come back to visit him at least once, but he never did.

I didn't hear from him at all. He was like a ghost that had vanished. My life was different, and I wasn't sure what had happened to it. I just knew that I needed to keep up with Ms Brittany. One day, I found her in her room having a hysterical time. Her phone had died, and she couldn't find it.

She nearly tore up the room looking for it. I helped her to look for it and we both were worn out searching. In this wild goose chase, we found a box of letters. The letters were handwritten letters from Robert. I asked her if I could borrow the box. She said, "Sure," not knowing what was in it. She was satisfied that I had found her the phone.

She listened to the message and asked me a habitual question that she would quickly forget.

"Rain?"

"Yes." I replied sitting next to her holding the box.

"Have you thought about giving your life to God?"

"Yes. I gave my life to God a few years ago when my youngest brother died."

"What happened to him?" I told her the story again of how my youngest brother was killed outside our apartment window. She cried a few tears and asked about me. It was both sincere and sweet. "Yes, I am doing much better. I was angry, and then I got really sad. It is hard to lose someone you love."

She nodded as she listened. "I remember going to his funeral. I heard the message about not wasting time. I didn't think I was wasting my time by being mad at God. I know it sounds silly, but I wanted to stay angry. I had two brothers who both died and a dad who stopped coming around. I didn't know and still don't if he is dead or alive."

"So, what did you do?"

"I went up to the pastor after the service. There

was no altar call, and I asked him, "How do I get right with God?"

"Did he tell you?"

"Yes, he told me I had to surrender to God. I remember thinking surrender what? I don't have anything else left. The pastor told me, I needed to surrender my pain and anger. He said it was dangerous for a person to hold anger in their heart because it will make us sin."

She nodded her head as she listened to me. I continued to say, "I can't remember the Bible verse he said, but then he told me. There are no perfect people, and we all fall short of the glory of God. We are all born sinners, and we need the grace of God to forgive us and change how we think. He asked me if I knew who Jesus was."

"What did you say?"

"I told him I knew of him, but didn't know him beyond the Bible stories I heard at church. He said to have a personal relationship with Yashua, another name for Jesus, you have to accept that he is the son of God, born of a woman. He is the Word of God, made to flesh, and he came to redeem the world. Anyone who believes in him shall not perish but will have everlasting life."

"Okay, yup. I heard that before," she replied.

"So I told him that I do believe that Yashua is

lord. I believe that the Word of God was made human, and he died for us to have healing from pain. I was hurting badly and I didn't know how to get rid of it. I didn't want to do drugs or something stupid; I knew that didn't work. The only way out was to be healed. And God healed my heart. I wasn't angry anymore, eventually and I started being able to smile again."

"So you did this prayer with the pastor, and you could release the pain you felt?"

"Yes. Having a personal relationship with God saved my life."

She sat there in silence for a little bit, and then she said, "Can you help me, I mean, talk to God and get me saved?" When she first asked me to pray with her, I was nervous. I honestly thought I would mess it up. I was scared that I messed it up. But every few days, we started having this conversation more.

I wondered where this conversation came from, but I figured it might have just been a long-standing memory that she liked to repeat. Later that day, when I went to go visit John. I brought the box. I was a bit late, but I was able to still see him. They scanned the letters, and I didn't think I was going to be able to give it to him, but I was.

"Thanks, Rain. I really appreciate you coming and checking on me. I know you won't be able to do this forever, and it is okay if you stop coming."

"Stop talking crazy. I would have been here sooner, but your mom lost her phone.

"Oh, yeah, that is her lifeline to dad. She would go berserk if she lost that."

"Yeah, we had a conversation after we found it, and it calmed her down."

"What was the conversation?"

"The norm. She asked me if I was saved and about my salvation story."

"She asked you about that?"

"Yeah, we talk about it all the time. At least two or three times a week."

John looked a little shocked. Which was interesting since nothing seemed to faze him nowadays. So I asked, "What?"

"Nothing, it's just, my mom wasn't saved. I mean she never went to an altar and gave her life to God. So you two talking about it is... different."

"Oh, I thought you knew."

"Knew what?"

"She gives her life to Christ every time she hears my story. We have done the prayer at least forty times. She has made me very comfortable with the

Romans Road. Yes, I do it my way, but I cover the basics."

"So, you telling me, my mom gets saved every week?"

"Yes." It took me a minute to get it to. Wow, she really wasn't saved. I thought he was joking, but he was serious. "You really didn't know?"

"No. Have you ever listened to the message my dad left my mom?"

"No, she keeps it on her ear when she hears it. I don't want to be rude, so I give her her privacy."

"You should listen to that message." Now curious, I plan to hear the message. "For the letters, I meant to tell you, we found those in your mom's room, when we were looking for the phone. I think they're from your dad."

"My dad?"

"Yeah, your mom didn't recognize the box, but I thought maybe you would know."

He thanked me again before it was time for him to be marched away in chains. It was the most nerve-wrecking sound imaginable. To know your feet and hands are not free to move how you want sounds unbearable. It was hard for my mom and my block going through the shock of all this. I was glad I didn't have to be home and deal with the long stares or judgment.

The only person I had to say something to was Keisha's Mom. She was a sweet lady, and I had nothing but love to share, but she turned her shoulder to me. She found out I was a witness to the crime, and she wasn't ready to forgive me for holding out on her. I couldn't explain all the moving parts, and I stopped trying. I just prayed about it, and I allowed her the room to be angry.

My mom told me that was all you could do when a mother loses her baby. Her pain will come breathing on anyone, and her breathing on John was the same thing. She wanted a trial and to see him go down in flames of agony. But looking at his condition, I knew that waving his trial was likely for the best. He grew ill, and one day, I found out just how bad it was when the nurse phoned me about his care.

"Rain Gray," she said on the other end.

"Yes, this is me," I replied unsure of what the call was for.

"I am calling you about an inmate at our facility. Do you have a moment to discuss this matter more?"

I replied, "Yes." I sat there and listened on the call as she explained numerous infections. She told me how some were controlled and others were not. They would do everything they could to restore his health, but with his condition, they are limited in resources and care at the facility. He really needed to be transferred to a more experienced facility, but there is a process to request to move him.

It was a hairy situation to throw in he still had legal issues pending, and they didn't want to move him until it was all finalized. I thought a confession was a closed book, but even a plea could take months to sort out. I wanted whatever was best for him and his condition, so I told her to do what she felt was necessary to make him well. She thanked me and hung up the phone.

I went to see him soon after that, and he was actually happy. I was surprised this time. I even thought some life came back to his face and body. I asked him when he sat down, "How's it going?"

"Good, they gave me the letters. And they were from my dad. I have been reading his journal, or letters to us over the years, and wow. I am not sure what happened to these letters, but I never got one. I am guessing James got them before either of us could, and hid them in that box."

"That is sad."

"Yeah, but Rain. He really did change. I know this sounds crazy coming from me. But he really did change." He starts to tear up and choke up. "I am reading the pages and it's like I can hear his heart in these pages. He really wanted to see all of us saved, you know?"

"Yeah, I can see that. Every believer wants to see their whole family saved."

"Hey you think, you think, you can help me get saved?"

"John, isn't there a pastor here?"

"Yeah, but I don't want everyone in my space like that. I trust you, Rain, you prayed for my mom."

"I can, I guess, you're the first person I know who will remember it, and I don't want to mess it up."

"You won't." I talk him through my version of the Romans Road. Through a thick sheet of glass, I saw John recite the Lord's prayer, and his eyes lit up. He had been reading, and I think he was already saved from his father's writings, but he wanted to do it with me also. I was honored and happy.

When the guard came, we both had more to say, and I meant to tell him about the medical stuff. I guess it would have to wait for our next visit. I went home to tell my mom, and at church, I gave the testimony too in my small group. I had joined a Bible club at church because I never had friends. With John away, I didn't have someone to spend time with besides my mother and Mrs. Brittany.

I loved them both, but I wanted to build my own relationships too. It was a good release to go weekly and talk about the Bible. I learned so much in Bible school, stuff I wouldn't have gotten just going to church. In fact, I learned more in 6 months of Bible school than going to church for the past few years.

It's not that what I studied I had never heard before, but I had never received it before. I needed to read it and study it, knowing what I know now. I needed this crazy time to pull me closer and create a thirst for me to seek Yah on my own. I would never ask that this be put on anyone, but being in this family forced me to read, study, and pray.

I sneaked and listened to the audio that Ms. Brittany listened to each day and night. It was a sweet and simple message. "Hey Babe. Things are getting better, and I believe God is going to save our boys and you, too. He is not through with me either. If I am not upstairs, I just fell asleep downstairs in front of the tv. I love you. Keep the bed warm, and I will have your food brought up."

Is this why she asks about being saved? But why now? This message is at least three years old. How can they not know she wanted to be saved, or got saved? Did the other cooks not mention it, or not see a reason to share it? I thought about that at night. I started sleeping in John's room when I semi-moved in to keep an eye on Mrs. Brittany. My mom still prefers to come and go home each night.

I think she is still concerned about her friend. I can't say I blame her. It can be lonely here sometimes, though. I see why John, felt so lonely in this big house. All these rooms but very few people to

talk to. It must have been hard on him. I went looking through his things, and I found portraits of all
his family at different times.

He really was a good painter, and you can tell
he loved it. I wanted to frame some of his work and
spread it more around the house. I remember looking at a picture of him, he looked like how I remembered him, and I thought to put him in the living
room near a portrait of his dad.

As I considered the placement, I heard the
phone ring. I stopped the party of thoughts in my
head, and I went to answer it. It was a call from the
correction facility, I accepted the charges, and I heard
John. "Rain," he was slow to speak, but I could hear
him. He hadn't been feeling too well, so the change
in his voice was normal. They were adjusting medi-
cations, and some could make him lethargic and blur
his speech.

"Hey John. How's the reading going?" I knew
not to ask how it was going. I could only imagine the
answer to be the same as before. Asking him about
the reading always made him happier, so I started
asking that question first before anything else. He replied, "Goo–d. I am just, just, trying to get things together. This med–icine has me a little jitte–jittery."

I knew this frustrated him as much as it would
anyone who knew what they wanted to say, and it
wouldn't come out. It was like he was recovering
from a stroke with how some of his movements
and words came out. "I just want–to tell you. Than-

thank you. Thank you, Rain."

"John, I don't mind, and you're welcome." Sometimes he does this, he will call me out of the blue, and won't ask for nothing, he just tells me thank you. At first, I didn't know what to say. Then I started saying how I felt. It got easier. "I love you, John, and I love your Mom. Don't worry, and just focus on taking care of yourself."

I could tell he nodded when he heard me. I don't know what it was, the medicine or the disease, but it came back with a vengeance when he left this house. Whatever they did in the prison, or the change in the environment, instantly had an impact on him. His health continued to deteriorate, but we hoped things with sentencing would speed up so he could get better care.

It was on a Sunday afternoon when I left church that I got a call from my mom. Before I could get good in the house, she said, "It's all over the news." I thought, "What now?" I looked and it was John. He had died the other night in his sleep from complications. It didn't say more. I saw the missed calls only after. When at church I turned my phone to silent, so I missed them all.

I was shattered. I couldn't breathe, I couldn't think, I couldn't smile, all I could do was cry. I cried for my friend, I cried for what could have been, I cried for what never happened. I was heartbroken because I thought that things wouldn't go this way.

He had it all: he had money, a mother who loved him, a father, a brother, and he was healthy. He had the life any child in the hood would have died to have. It wasn't perfect, but he was loved even though he might not have felt it all the time.

I don't know what took a dive, but in months of knowing him, I learned to love him, and I know he loved me. The love we shared for each other was real, but now it is gone. I didn't know what to do with the broken pieces of my heart.

THE GREATEST WITNESS

I was broken for weeks. I was losing weight, and my mom had to come and see about me. I felt silly to be falling apart, but I tried to keep it together. The funeral was silent. He didn't have many friends, and I wasn't sure of inviting his mother. She was already struggling, and I wasn't sure of how she would respond to seeing John gone.

I decided not to show her him the way he was. He was very skinny and not like himself. His eyes were sunken, and his body frail. It was not the way I wanted to remember him either, so I said no to leaving the casket open during the service. It was a simple service with my pastor and those who came to support me.

It was a hard day for me, and my mom was the one who got me through it, so I could be there for Mrs. Brittany. It was very hard to smile and be normal around her because I didn't want to lie to her. I was trying to get back in the groove of things, but it was hard. I did get one surprise visitor who I didn't recognize at the funeral.

He didn't say anything, but he sat in the back of the church and kept to himself. He was in a wheelchair, and he wasn't anyone I had noticed before. I didn't

think anything of it until I saw him again at the buri-
al site. I went up to him, but keeping my distance, I
asked, "Excuse me, did you know John?"

He turned around and I knew his face. He was
James. We didn't say anything for a moment, but we
stared at each other. Tears were running down his face,
and I knew he had been the guy in the church, too; he
came.

I wondered if he would come. I thought he would
because I knew his brother made the news, and he
would see it. I just believed that God would bring them
full circle somehow. He invited me to have a cup of
coffee with him, and I agreed. We sat there in the park,
silent at first.

I was going to speak, but then he beat me to it and
said, "I really owe you an apology, Rain. If my brother
were here, I would say I owe him one, too. I just–I just
thought I had enough time…" He started crying. I could
feel the hurt and pain in his voice. I didn't know his
story, but I was curious. What happened to him?

How did a cold killer get here? What was the story? He cleared his throat and said, "I tried to get here
sooner. I wanted to see him before something like this
happened. I had a bad feeling, but I wasn't in a good
place, Rain. I am so sorry." I heard him, and it seemed
right to give him a hug, so I did.

He cried for several moments. Like his brother,
he didn't need me to say anything. So I didn't. I let him
cry. He regained his composure after a while and said,
"I owe you, Rain. My whole family owes you. Whatever
you need, I will give it to you. Just let me know."

"No, no. I don't need anything. John took care of all that."

"You see, even when I should do something for him. I am the older brother, he already did it for me. I was never smart like him. I never got to do great in school and stuff like that. I struggled. The streets was what I had. It made me something, or at least I thought it did."

He wiped his tears a bit more and said, "But I was a monster. I ran off everyone who could have loved me. I didn't see what John was trying to tell me, my Mom, or my Dad. I just saw me. It took God, Rain, it took God for me to see me." He took another moment, and I saw his lip quivering. I know whatever he saw or experienced was enough to change his life forever.

"When I saw my brother last, he told me he loved me and that family stays no matter what. He said he would be here for me and would take care of it. I told him he was a–I don't really talk like that no mo'. BI was made because of you and the shooting. I called him names and I left Rain. I got in my car and I left him."

James' Flashback...

"This can't be happening. I told him. That bitches only lead to jail or death. They don't mean you no good. What did he say? I love Rain." I talked to myself in that car for hours as I drove to I don't know where. I didn't have any place to go. I couldn't use my cards, I took some cash, but I had to move quickly so I couldn't get no big money to reset like I wanted to.

The biggest asset I had was my car. I didn't have

anything else. I was thinking how could he be so stupid to pick a woman over me. I mean I thought he was gay. So, how? How does he pick that bitch over me.

Back to today...

"My apologies, Rain, I am not this dude no more. But I was pissed about you." I nodded my head in understanding to hear him out. He continued.

James' Flashback...

I was angry and I had been doing 90 on the highway. My head was in the clouds, and it was only the grace of God that I didn't get pulled over. I wasn't high or nothing. But when he told me what he had planned to do, I didn't have long to make a decision. I could either pursue finding Rain, but what difference would it make if he was gonna turn himself in?

I kept driving because I was mad and I felt helpless. We built all this, and now it is crumbling down. First hit was my mother. Then my father, and now my brother could get a life sentence.

I thought we should try and beat it and pay people off, but he told me, his way was best. I played this conversation in my head as I drove. I slowed down, but I didn't slow down fast enough, and I nearly hit a car. That woke me up and told me to get off the highway. I don't know what town I was in, but it was a small town. It looked like farmland.

It seemed like it was grass everywhere I looked. I must have drove through to the next morning because the sky was going from dark to some light. I was

242

driving, but I was still heavily in thought. The same thoughts that had me distracted on the highway, had me distracted on the streets.

I was driving and I missed my turn. It was still a bit dark, so I thought I could just turn a wide turn and go back the other way. The dark still covered the ground, and I didn't know that where I planned my u-turn was a small drop off. The car landed sideways but on top of a tree stump that jammed through the car. It was like I landed on a harpoon stick.

I blanked out, screaming for help. I didn't know what had happened. All I remember was black. Then I heard a voice come near me, "Hey! Hey! Can you hear me?"

"Yeah, I can hear you. Help me get the fuck out of here." I remember me saying. The voice was calm and he said, "I can help you, but I have to first get you unstuck."

He continued to talk and said, "Do you know what happened?"

"I was trying to turn around because I missed my turn," I replied in a curt way. I just don't like being asked dumb questions; clearly, I made a bad judgment call, so I am in a ditch. I didn't realize he was trying to keep me talking, so I didn't panic or pass out. I was in and out. But the guy who started to talk to me kept talking to me until the tow truck came and a paramedic.

When they arrived, the bright lights and noise did something to me, and this time I saw a white light.

Then nothing. I heard nothing, saw nothing. It was like being exposed to too much light, and your eyes are trying to adjust. When my eyes adjusted, I woke up–or I thought I did. I heard a voice say to me, with no face, "Where are you going, James?"

I replied, "Anywhere. I don't got a home."

"But James, family stays together and looks out for each other."

"My family ain't no family." I was rude and mad. I wasn't sure at who or why, but I was boiling over.

"You need to let go of that anger, James. It won't help none."

"Why? Because you said so?"

"Because I know what's good for you."

"Really, how? Who are you, God?" And just like that, I woke up. I heard the voice I remembered, but the man didn't look familiar. He was a black older man, wearing farming clothes, I guess. He seemed friendly, but I didn't know him. He said, "Hey? How you do-ing?"

"I was just in a car accident. How the hell do you think I am doing?"

"I would say you are doing better now. Do you know your name?"

"Why wouldn't I know my name? It's, It's James."

"Okay, James. You have been in the hospital for a little over three days. I found you in a bad wreck and had the paramedics bring you here. You got any family that would be looking for you?"

"No, but I can take care of myself. I don't need them." I replied firmly.

"I think you are going to rethink that. You are gonna need some help."

"I told you I don't need no dame help."

The older man got up from the bed and said. "Well, look, if you change your mind and fix your attitude, you can come by my place until you get on your feet. You were a little tossed about, and without legs you are gonna struggle to get around by yourself."

I almost laughed at the man. "What the hell you mean no legs? I got legs right here." I looked down and yanked the blanket off. My jaw dropped, and I start wiggling my nubs back and forth, trying to feel my toes. I tried to feel my knees; my feet, and they were all gone. I said with fury, "What the hell happened to my dame legs?"

"Okay, I am a man of God. You ain't gonna keep cursing at me. If you calm down, I will go over this one more time. You lost your legs in your accident when you went off the cliff."

"Man, this is not funny. If this is some sick dream, this is twisted shit, and I don't like it. This isn't real. I just dreamed a voice was talking to me, and now you talking about my legs is gone? And I have been sleep for three days?"

"Like I said, I gotta go. I got a room for you down at the church if you need a place to stay. I help rehabilitate people when they are in a tough spot. If you need me, I can help you."

"I don't need your dame help. I got money. I am good."

"If you got this covered. I will leave. If you change your mind, the nurses have my information." The man turned around and was gone. I was there sitting in the bed, looking at my hotel for the past three days and in my condition. I had plans to go to a hotel and figure stuff out. This wasn't part of the plan.

Losing my legs is taken away my ability to drive or do anything for myself. I minus well be a vegetable, I thought as I lay there. I was kept at the hospital another four days before they were ready to kick me out. Problem, I didn't have anything. All of my items were in the car, and who knows what happened to them.

My biggest asset now had a tree stump piercing through it, I was broke, and homeless. What was I gonna do now? I knew I had to call the old man back. I couldn't get anywhere like this, not even home. I couldn't get back home even if I wanted to. I was stuck wherever God put me.

That old man came and got me and he got me right real quick. When he came, I said, "I don't need you for long. Just long enough for me to get my shit together, than I will be gone."

He promptly replied, "If you keep cussing at me, you will get your stuff together today, and you will not be coming with me. I am not your homie, your friend, I am a man of God trying to help you. Now, do you understand what I am asking?"

I took a deep breath and said, "Yes, I understand. No problem." He pushed me out of the hospital and brought me to this church. It was other guys there also who like me was abandoned or straight out of jail. At this church, we had so many rules. It was like I went to prison.

We had a set time for getting up, had chores, had to clean, and even go to church. He didn't tell me at the hospital that I had to go to church. Not sure it would have made much of a difference, but at least I could have been ready for it. I probably would have come up with an excuse and fought harder not to come, although I am not sure why.

I needed God, but I didn't know that when I came. I was a grump for about the first month I was there. I was mad about my legs. Mad about my money. The food, the shelter, the living quarters. It was all less than I expected out of life. I have never had to do for myself. We always had someone do that for us. Here, we had to do it for ourselves.

I learned how to cook, wash clothes, fold, and do other house chores. I thought he was joking since I had no legs, but he wasn't. Not having legs didn't mean I got to do less, or do nothing. I thought it would be a cake walk to come to that church and live to work through the crap in my head. Every day it was a new challenge physically, emotionally, and eventually spiritually for me.

I remember he asked me one day, "What has been so wrong with your life that has you so angry?"

I just looked at him and didn't say nothing. I knew I couldn't cuss, without that I felt square trying to answer him. It wasn't me. I felt I was getting soft and didn't like it. I needed my edge. So he asked again, "So what, did you come from a well-off family that gave you everything?"

"Gave me? My family ain't give me sh–nothing. I earned everything I ever had. Not all of it was rightfully earned, but I paid the price. Nothing was given to me."

"Alright, so why are you mad? We all gotta work to make a living. Even here, you gotta work to stay."

"Yeah, but this is different."

"Alright, how so?"

"I asked to be here. I didn't ask for how I grew up."

"We don't get the chance to pick our parents, Son. We just have to be grateful we are here."

"Even if we came from drug dealing murderous parents?"

"Even if. The Bible is clear to obey our parents so our days can be long. That means we are to respect them, we don't have to agree or follow in their ways. When you are young, you might not have much of a

248

choice, but when you can choose, you can make the choice on what you will do. Aren't you a grown man now?"

"Yes,"

"Then you have a choice to make. You can choose how you live your life."

"But it has always been my dad's–"

"Is your dad here?"

"No."

"So, is it your dad's choice or your choice?"

"You don't understand, I learned his ways. They're not so easy to just get rid of."

"You're right, you have to train yourself, be patient, and allow yourself to grow. Stop beating yourself up. We all make mistakes. No matter who we are. God has helped murderers, rapists, thieves, liars, prostitutes, and many others get there lives in order–and these are people from the Bible. He can help you too, when you're ready."

I tried to argue with what he said, and he would tell me. "You don't believe me. Let me show you this right here about..." And he would walk me through the Bible for each of them. I thought people in the Bible was supposed to be perfect examples. I mean I knew they were flawed, I just didn't think they were flawed like me.

One by one, he taught me about people in the Bible. I went to church for months before I started to really get what God was showing me. He was calling me, but I was running from Him. I was running from healing, from seeing my true condition. I thought I was good, I just needed my legs back. But the truth is, losing my legs was the best thing that could have happened to me. I got what John wanted to do. He wanted to stop running.

Back to day...

I sat there, choked up but fighting to keep my composure. It was so humbling and a world's apart difference from what I saw months ago. I saw what God could do, and it was powerful. He really did something to James' heart, and I am a witness.

He then said, "That old man was good to me. He showed me what I was too hot-headed to let my dad show me. I couldn't accept it from him because he was the largest reason I became a monster. My mom was no better. For me, she wanted a jar head, but from my brother, she just wanted him to be alive. I was jealous of him, Rain."

He continued, "I wanted to be him, but he didn't want to be me. He wanted to be something bigger than me. I didn't know what it was, and I was jealous of that, too. He wanted out, and I wanted a partner in this thing with me. I wanted to not be alone. My fear was to be alone, and here I am, Rain, alone."

"But you are not alone. I am here. God is here. And although your brother can't tell you, he never stopped believing in you. He was willing to lay down

250

his life so you could have one. He knew this day would come when I didn't. I didn't think you were ever gonna come around."

"I know. I thought that too. But you stayed here, taking care of my mom and my brother. I owe you."

"But my prayer was for you to come and be with your family. Your mother needs you. You are all she has left. You should make time to see her. I didn't let her come to the funeral, so you have to come by the house."

"Yeah. That was for the best. She might of freaked out seeing me."

"I think you might be surprised. You should see your mom." A few moments later, the Old Man came up and introduced himself. "Hi, I am Cecil. I've been helping to take care of James."

I shook his hand and thanked him. It was nice to meet the man who was patient enough to win the soul of James to Christ! I never thought I would see the day, but the day was here and I was glad to see it. I knew that John was smiling down from heaven to see it too and their father, Robert.

It was a bittersweet moment for sure, but he needed to come home. They followed me back to the house, and I tried to alert Brittany of their coming. She was puzzled, but when she saw him, she didn't freak out or run. She came up to him and gave him a big hug and said, "John, where have you been? What happened to your legs?"

He tried to tell her his name, but she wasn't listening. She named him John, and that's what she kept calling him. She wanted him to stay, but he said he couldn't but would come back often. It was a deep cry that he had to get a hug from his mother. She didn't know his name, but whatever spirit was on John was on James, and she could see it.

Before he left, I slipped some cash into his pocket for making things easier for him in the future. I also gave him a card to use whenever he needed anything. I got a huge settlement check for when John passed. Robert was a smart man and so was Brittany is all I could say. They got life insurance policies on everyone. So when the dad passed, they got a lump sum. When John passed, I got a lump sum and the trust.

James had money left for him too by his father and brother. I was guardian over it, so he didn't blow it. I took John's place on the trust. I don't know how things changed the way they did, but I knew this was the beginning of something great. I knew we would find a way to push forward.

MUCH IS GIVEN MUCH IS REQUIRED

I remembered as I sat on the beach from the promise I made to my mom. "Mom, I don't know how, but we are going to save up and make it to Jamaica." When I said that I had no clue of what all it would take to buy us time here on the island. I had no idea who would be joining us on this excursion, either. To bring along friends and turn enemies into Kingdom Ambassadors of Christ, was one I never thought about.

I never knew that a job lost would equal a life of family and growth gained. I learned to trust God in everything, because what can look like the devil or even be evil, in the hands of God can be turned around for our good. There is a scripture that says God will turn everything to our good.

As I twiddle my toes in the sand and watch the waves, I see my mom smiling back at me. She could retire any day now, but she chooses to work with Mrs. Brittany. No longer for pay, but to keep her life comfortable. She travels with her and makes sure that things are good and right for her.

She knows her best, and with her traveling, we are able to get her out of the house more. For James, he took his money and decided to partner with the pastor, Cecil. He and the Old Man have a powerful ministry to rehabilitate men after experiencing a great loss, coming out of jail, or undergoing a life change.

He comes and sees his mother often and she calls him affectionately, John. He has learned to love it. Maybe someday she will come him, James, to his surprise and mine.

Keisha's Mom came with us to Jamaica. She is still uncertain of how she feels about us as a family, but she has accepted our olive branch. I am believing for God to continue this great work of restoration. Even if she is not ready, I couldn't give up on wanting to make things right, however I could. John never gave up on James, so I didn't want to give up on Keisha's Mom and the power of God to change things.

As for me, I enjoy living a life with people who have become family. I gained two brothers. I love John, and will always love James too. I never thought I would grow to like James, let alone love or see him as family. I didn't think I could. But God showed me what he could do in me, too. Is there really anything too big or hard for God?

ABOUT THE AUTHOR

"God blesses those who work for peace, for they will be called the children of Yah (God)." Matthew 5:9

Dr. Lee has authored over thirty books across more than seven genres: adult, children, youth fiction, self-help, spiritual growth, novels, business, empowerment, etc. to help people in their most profound times of need.

She is also passionate about coaching programs and web courses she created for WAE (Write Anything Easily) Process, Embrace Your Crown, Turn Key Solution for Small and New Businesses, Transform Go Beyond Change (Personal Development, and The Lesson for youth and teenagers.

Connect and Shop my books:

AuthorKLee.com

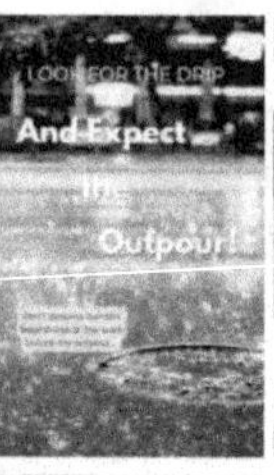

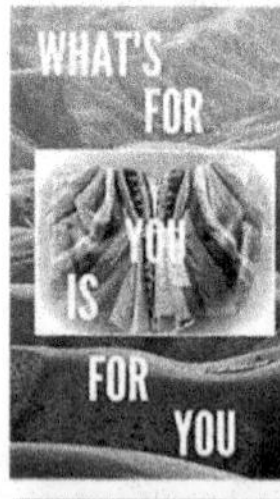

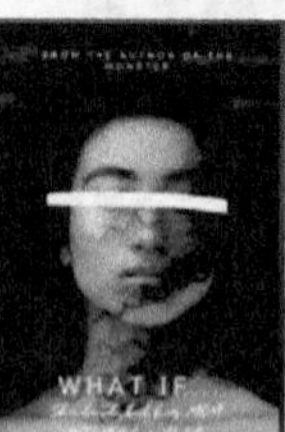

AuthorKLee.com Creator of *WAE Proces*

Explore over seven different book genres, and find something suitable for every member of the family.

SCAN ME

Call or Text:
770-240-0089 Press Extension 1
Web: KLEpub.com
Email Services@klepub.com

It's time to start and finish   **YOUR Story!**

KLE Publishing specializes in helping people become authors. In as little as 15 to 90 days, we can help you develop your books and e-books and publish to 39,000 outlets! We also offer audiobook services.

Write, Edit, Format, Publish
We can help from
Start to Finish.

KLE Publishing Books

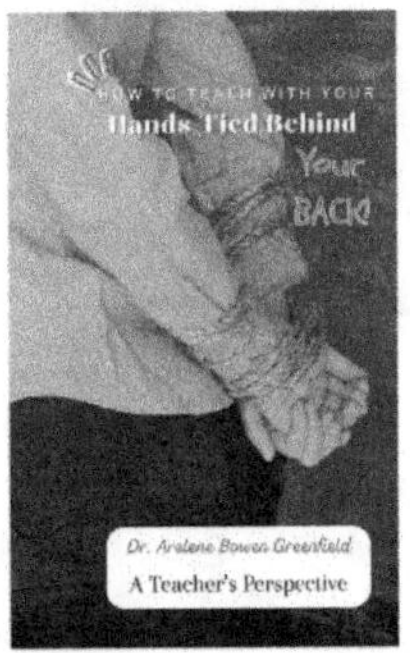

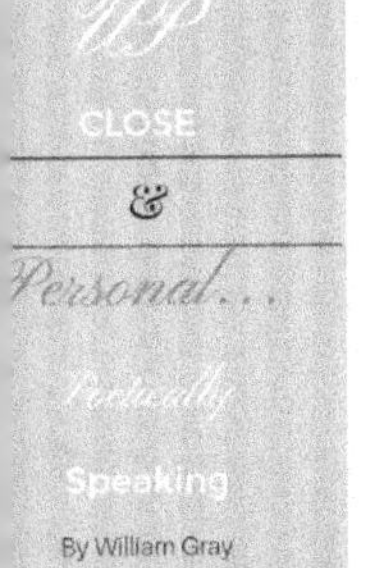